LOSS
BOOK 1

RECOVERY

ALASKAN SECURITY-TEAM ROGUE

Jemma
WESTBROOK

Loss Recovery, book 1 in the Alaskan Security-Team Rogue series.
Copyright 2019 by Jemma Westbrook.
www.jemmawestbrook.com

First printing, 2019
Cover design by Robin Harper at Wicked by Design.

CHAPTER 1

"YOU READY TO be back in the cold?"

Wade turned his attention from the small airplane window to where his closest friend sat beside him. "Not everyone likes Florida as much as your crazy ass does."

He and Brock just spent the past four weeks on the Gulf coast, making sure the daughter of a smuggler didn't end up paying the ultimate price for what her father chose to do with his free time.

It was four weeks too long.

Brock leaned back in his leather seat on Alaskan Security's smallest jet, lifting one shoulder as he took a sip of his beer. "My love of Florida has nothing to do with the weather, though." He shot Wade a grin. "You don't get to see near as much skin in Alaska." He started to tip his beer back again but stopped, eyes focusing on Wade. "Not that you took advantage of it."

LOSS RECOVERY

Wade glared long and hard at Brock before turning back to look out at the snow-covered landscape getting closer with each passing second. "Not everyone is as driven by their dick as you are."

Brock scoffed in mock offense. "You wound me."

Wade didn't bother responding. Brock meant well. His friend had tried everything to get him out of this funk for almost two years.

That meant two years of Brock showing up at their hotel rooms with women. Two years of him dragging Wade to every bar they passed. Hell, at one point Brock even made him a fake Tinder account trying to get him to hook up with someone.

Wade wasn't interested in any of it.

"You look over the file yet?" Thankfully, Brock must have realized it was time to move the conversation along.

It was why they were still friends. Brock knew to push just far enough, and then back off before Wade had to be a dick.

"No." He barely glanced at the manila envelope as it fell into his lap. It didn't really matter what was inside. Who he was protecting. This job no longer held the excitement it once did.

The shine had worn off. Wiped away by the knowledge of what it stole from him.

What he could never have because of it.

"You should probably at least read it over before we get there. Might give the wrong impression if you don't know what the fuck's going on." Brock's tone was sharper now, showing his growing irritation with the perpetual bad mood Wade always wore. "Might make this woman doubt your ability to protect her if you don't know who the fuck you're supposed to be keeping away."

Wade snatched the file. "It's not fucking rocket science." He flipped open the file, pausing as Brock's words sank in. "Her?" He scanned the top sheet of information. "I thought it was a man." He found the name he remembered. "Roger Hines."

"That's who hired us, but it was to protect his daughter." Brock ran a finger down the page until it rested just below another name. "Bessie Hines."

"Another prick doing shit to put his family in danger?" It was a lucrative business they were in, offering protection to people who didn't always deserve it.

Unfortunately, it was also a business model Wade was struggling with more and more. It's why he'd been pushing Shawn to assign him and Brock to jobs like the one in Florida. It was a way for him to lean a little more to the right side of the wrong line he walked.

Brock shook his head. "Dude, this is why you've gotta fucking read the files." He flipped to the next page of the stack of papers in the file. "She's got a restraining order against some dick she used to date."

Wade stared down at the court record in front of him. "Does that say kidnapping?"

"You're the one reading it." Brock polished off the last of his beer. "Finally."

"Ass." Wade scanned the list of charges against Chris Snyder. "Have you read this shit?"

Brock snorted. "Of course I've fucking read it." He shook his head. "Some men don't like to take no for an answer I guess."

"He's going to have to learn how." Wade straightened in his seat, feeling just a little like he used to. Maybe because he finally had a job that felt like it mattered.

Like it would make a fucking difference.

Sure they kept the girl in Florida safe. Knocked out a few shitty humans in the process, ridding the world of their presence. But at the end of the day it didn't matter. Her father wasn't going to quit doing what he was doing, and it was only a matter of time before she ended up on another bad guy's radar.

Ricardo's voice came over the speaker. "Sit your asses down. We're about to land."

Brock leaned to the left, yelling toward the open door to the cockpit. "You don't have to use that thing, asshole. We can hear you."

The hollow sound of an open connection came across the speaker a second before their pilot's voice. "Kiss my ass, Brock. I like it. Makes me feel professional."

"Professional my ass." Brock flipped the file on Wade's lap closed and shoved it into his bag. "Is it just teams of two on this one?"

"Shawn hasn't said different." He and Brock were always partnered up, but depending on the situation, Shawn occasionally added another man

8

to the teams they normally worked in. "Want me to ask Ricardo to join us?"

"I'll kill you and make it look like an accident." Brock's body jumped around a little as the plane touched down. He grabbed the seat in front of him and leaned into the aisle again. "That's not fucking funny, Rico."

Ricardo's deep laugh was loud enough to be heard over the sound of the air fighting the wing flaps as the plane slowed.

Brock's well-tanned skin paled as he gripped his bag to his chest. "Tell him that's not fucking funny."

"Don't give him shit and he won't give you shit." Wade grabbed his own bag and slung it over his shoulder as the plane made its way toward the small terminal of the tiny private airport where Alaskan Security stored their planes. He glanced out the window to see the rolling stairs were already out, being shoved into place by—

Wade squinted at the man stomping his way across the tamarack. "Is that Shawn?"

Brock leaned in beside him. "What the fuck is Shawn doing out there?"

The plane came to a stop and Ricardo stepped through the doorway of the cockpit, black brows pushed together as he opened the door. "What the fuck is Shawn doing?"

As soon as the door was open Shawn rushed through. He pointed at Brock and Wade. "Come on. We gotta go."

Wade stepped past Brock. "What's wrong?"

9

"Your lady showed up a day early and wasn't real happy we weren't ready for her." Shawn shook his head a little. "That one is going to be a handful."

"Great." Brock grabbed his coat and followed Wade out of the plane and down the steps. "Nothing worse than a woman who's all wound up."

"Her ex-boyfriend is going schizo and the people her parents hired to keep her safe didn't show up. I would say she has the right to be a little wound up."

Wade dropped his bag to the ground and shoved his arms into his black down-lined parka. The air here felt colder after spending so long in the heat of Florida, and the chill was already biting into his skin.

"She wasn't supposed to be here until tomorrow." Brock fought on his own coat as they kept walking to the black SUV waiting for them. "It's not our fault she showed up a day early."

"Doesn't matter. She's probably scared shitless if she was willing to move here to hide from him." Wade opened the door and climbed into the back seat, the heated interior already a welcome relief. He was getting soft. Maybe he'd sit outside naked for a while. Build his tolerance back up.

It was one of the main reasons they were the only security company in the state. No one else could handle the frigid temperatures.

It was also one of the main reasons their income was so lucrative and their schedule was so full. The cold meant less people and fewer cops. In

Alaska you could virtually disappear. Good for the woman they were on their way to meet.

But also good for criminals looking to hide out.

Shawn jumped into the driver's seat and immediately pulled away. "How was the flight?"

"Fine." Wade settled back in his seat. "Where is she at?"

"I set her up in number five. Figured she deserved the nicest we had to offer since we dropped the ball."

Wade caught Shawn's eyes in the rearview mirror. "*We* dropped the ball?"

"Her father sent an email letting me know he was putting her on the next plane. Apparently there was an incident."

Fuck. No wonder this woman was upset. "What kind of an incident?"

"He came to her house. Stood just outside the reach of the security cameras so she couldn't prove he was there."

They didn't deal with too many domestic cases. Most of what they did leaned more toward the jobs that no one else would take, either because of the questionable dealings of the client, or because the threat of violence was more of a guarantee.

It was why they could charge what they did. The people they protected had the money to pay it and no other options.

But this woman would have multiple options available to her. Anyone would have taken her case on.

"Why did they hire us?" Brock voiced the thought working its way through Wade's head.

Shawn looked at them long and hard in the mirror. "I think you know the answer to that. He wants his daughter safe." Shawn paused just long enough. "At any cost."

They weren't mercenaries.

Technically.

But if the opportunity arose to take out someone who needed taking out, Team Rogue was more than happy to do the world a favor.

Wade gave Shawn a nod. "Fair enough."

Brock leaned forward. "You have our phones?"

"Everything's in the back." Shawn turned the SUV onto the narrow road leading to one of the ten safe-houses in the small town of Brisbane that Alaskan Security called home. "I grabbed you some clothes, but you might have to get more between shifts."

While out-of-state jobs were all work all the time, most local jobs were done with two-man teams, each working in ten-hour blocks before switching out.

Unless shit was going bad. Then it was all hands on deck, all the time.

As long as nothing went wrong, this would be a nice break after working around-the-clock for a month.

Number five came into view as the Rover bumped down the snow-covered drive. It was the largest of the cabins Alaskan Security owned, with six bedrooms and a large, open kitchen sporting high-end appliances. Usually it was reserved for either their highest paying jobs, or the most dangerous, where multiple guards were required to be on hand at all times. "How many men are on this?"

"Just two at a time." Shawn's gaze didn't meet his in the mirror. "For now."

Wade started to ask what the fuck that meant, but Shawn cut him off, throwing the SUV into park and jumping out. "I'll introduce you. Then I've got to go. Got another job I gotta get lined up before someone dies."

"Wouldn't want that to happen, now would we?" Wade didn't even try to keep the disdain out of his tone. He used to look at this job differently. Used to think it didn't matter who he protected, as long as he was successful.

Now he wasn't so sure.

Shawn started up the shoveled sidewalk toward the porch, but stopped suddenly, turning to face them, his eyes trained on Wade. "Be nice to her. She's been through a lot."

"What the fuck is that supposed to mean?"

Shawn's head tipped to one side. "Come on, man. I heard you made Courtney cry."

"She was being fucking ridiculous." He wasn't being paid to go buy a twenty-year-old eyeliner at ten at night. "Someone was trying to kill her and she was treating us like her assistants."

Shawn let out a long breath. "Listen. I know lately you've been feeling a little…"

"Pissy." Brock finished the sentence before wrapping his arm around Shawn and turning him back toward the house. "He'll be fine."

That wasn't true. Wade hadn't been fine in almost two years.

Because two years ago he had a taste of all he was missing and it changed everything.

One night and one woman had turned his whole world upside down and then set it on fire, leaving him to live in the burned-out remains of what might have been.

He followed them up the steps and onto the covered porch where Shawn rang the bell before punching in the code to unlock the door. He and Brock walked in first, leaving Wade to close and lock the door behind them.

When Wade turned around the woman occupying cabin number five was standing in the middle of the vaulted great room staring at him, her full lips barely parted, her hazel eyes wide.

She was just as perfect as she was two years ago. Just as beautiful as the night she lit the match that incinerated his life.

Wade took a step, blinking hard, thinking he had to be wrong.

It couldn't be her. Not here.

But then she said a name. The name only one woman had ever called him. "Whitt?"

It was a fake name. A way to ensure she would never be able to find him if she decided to look. Bringing people into his life wasn't an option. It was too dangerous.

But here she was. Brought to him by her own demons.

Wade took another step toward her. He barely glanced at Brock and Shawn, shoving one finger toward the door. "Get out."

Carly—

No.

The woman he knew as Carly softly gasped as one hand went over her mouth. "This can't be happening."

Wade knew he wasn't the only one who used a fake name that night. For two years he wondered what her name really was.

Now he knew. It wasn't Carly Smith like she claimed. It was Bessie Hines.

It fit her so much better.

Wade dragged his eyes from Bess to glare at the two men still standing beside him. "I said get out. Now."

"Are you seri—"

"Out." He didn't wait for them to stall any longer. Wade grabbed Brock by the shoulder of his coat and pulled him toward the door. "I'll call you later."

He shoved the two men out the door and relocked it, taking a breath before turning back to the woman who changed his whole life in one night.

She stood perfectly still, one delicate hand covering her mouth, almost green eyes still wide with shock. She barely shook her head. "What are you doing here?"

Wade started walking toward her. "Your father hired me to protect you." His steps came faster, eating up the remaining space between them. Even then it felt like it took him forever to get to her.

Because it *had* taken him forever to get to her.

He grabbed her, pulling Bess tight against him, burying his face in her hair, never considering she might not feel like he did.

That she might not have thought about him every night like he had her.

That she didn't wish every minute of every day that things could be different.

That he hadn't left.

Bess. Her name was Bess.

And she was here. With him.

Finally.

She collapsed against him, her small frame falling into his arms. "I can't believe this."

He held her close, breathing in the unforgettable scent of her skin. He'd searched everywhere trying to find it, needing something to remind him that she was real, that she had been his, even if it was only for one night, but never once did Wade find anything even close to the warm jasmine scent filling his lungs.

Her soft body suddenly went still in his arms, stiffening until she slowly pushed from his embrace. He let her go, even though it was the hardest thing he'd ever done. He'd waited so long, never thinking he would see her again.

Always praying he would. That the same twist of fate that pulled them together once would do it again.

And it had.

But maybe Bess couldn't forgive him for leaving her the way he did. Maybe what they shared hadn't meant to her what it did to him.

Wade held perfectly still, waiting.

Bess took a shaky breath. "I have to tell you something."

"Is it about Chris?" He took a step closer, needing to be near her even if he couldn't touch her. "I don't care who you've been with, Bess. It doesn't matter."

That was a lie. It did matter who she'd been with, but only because now Wade would have to kill the bastard who dared to hurt her. Chris Snyder had worse things to worry about than prison now. Now he should pray for the safety of a jail cell. It was all that would protect Bessie's ex from the hell coming for him.

Bess shook her head, the long blonde hair Wade dreamed of almost every night swinging over her shoulders. "I haven't been with anyone." Her voice dropped to a whisper. "Not since you."

Wade stilled. "Who is Chris then?"

He should have listened to Brock. If he'd looked at her file he would know everything. Would know how much he would have to punish the man who hurt her.

"He's my ex."

Wade tried to catch up. Tried to remember everything he knew of her.

"The one from when we met?" He knew she was trying to break free of someone. Find her way from a bad relationship. It was what drove her to him no doubt, and he'd been grateful as hell.

But now he didn't feel the same.

Two years and this guy was still chasing her? Not just chasing, but stalking. Assaulting.

Kidnapping.

Rage fired through him, hot and angry. Anger at fucking Chris Snyder.

But mostly at himself.

Because he knew Bess was different after just one night with her, and he should never have left. He should have stayed. Done what he wanted to do in spite of how wrong he convinced himself it was.

Fuck the consequences.

Wade tried to reach for her again but Bess stepped back, away from his touch.

Still out of his reach.

He took a step toward her but one small palm came up between them, stopping him dead in his tracks. "Stop." Her tone was strong, unwavering. "I—"

A sound from the first-floor bedroom cut her off.

The sound of a baby crying.

CHAPTER 2

"SHIT." BESS SPUN away, rushing from the room.

She hurried to the portable crib one of the men from the security company her parents hired brought in for Parker to sleep in. "It's okay." She scooped him up, cradling his little body against hers as she pressed a kiss to the dark hair on his head, breathing in his smell, trying to ease the rapid fire of her heart.

This was a moment she never thought would come. Even in this digital age filled with personal data and internet and DNA, she'd never been able to find him.

And she'd tried.

"Bess?"

The sound of her name in his voice sent a wave of warmth rippling through her. It was something she'd imagined more times than she could count on the long lonely nights sitting in a rocking chair, holding her baby.

Possibly their baby.

"Yes?"

"That's a baby."

She nodded. "It is."

"How old is..." The man she knew as Whitt stepped in beside her. "He?"

"He." She turned, making herself look up at him, trying to find the same bravery she felt that night so long ago. "What is your name?" Bess qualified the request. "Your *real* name?"

"Wade." He reached out to touch one finger to Parker's shoulder, stroking the fuzzy fabric of his footed pajamas. "Denison." His eyes hadn't left Parker since he walked into the large bedroom. "What's his name?"

"Parker." She stood silently as Wade stared at the baby she held, gently touching his arms. His back.

"How old is he?" The question was barely a whisper. So soft it was impossible to tell what Wade was hoping to hear.

"Fourteen months." The math was simple to do, but only if he remembered when they met.

And based on his reaction to seeing her, Wade very much remembered. It was a fact she refused to let herself spend too much time on.

Wade's dark gaze immediately snapped to hers. "He's mine."

It wasn't a question. "I think so."

"Think?" Wade's eyes were back on Parker. "We could find out."

It's what she'd prayed for every night as she tried to find sleep. That somehow, some way, she would find this man. Prove Chris wasn't Parker's father without risking what would happen if she was wrong.

Because there was a slim chance she might be. But any chance was too much when it came to Parker's safety. "Could we go now?"

Wade's attention lifted to her. He barely shook his head. "Not now. Not yet." He shifted closer, the hands that had been on her son, coming to rest on her face, cradling her cheeks with the same soft touch Bess was sure she remembered as being genuine.

But after two years she'd begun to doubt herself. Question the truth of her memories of the night they spent together.

It couldn't have been all she thought. He couldn't have been as handsome. As gentle.

The connection she thought they had couldn't have been real.

It was one night. A single interaction. How could it have meant as much as it seemed like it did?

And it wasn't just because it might have created her son. Even if nothing else had come of that night, Bess would still be right where she was.

Wishing for something impossible.

But the look in Wade's eyes made her hope that maybe it wasn't as impossible as she thought.

And that was freaking terrifying.

"I never thought I would see you again." His eyes closed.

She waited for him to say something else. To explain why he never tried to find her.

Because he could have. Bess didn't know enough about him to go on, but Wade definitely knew enough to find her. He knew where she lived. That her family owned a very large and very well-known construction company. Finding her would have taken five minutes.

And he hadn't done it.

"Why didn't you try to find me?" The question sounded weak. Accusatory.

And damn it, maybe it should.

Two years she'd been alone. Pregnant. Scared of a man who believed the baby she was carrying had to be his.

Wade could have fixed it all before—

Before it came to what it had.

"I'm not the kind of man a woman should want, Bess. I knew if I found you I wouldn't have been able to stay away."

"Not the kind of man—" She stepped back, suddenly feeling the anger that had flashed a few times over the months she'd been alone. "Do you have any idea what kind of man I've been dealing with?" Her chin threatened to quiver and she bit her tongue, trying to keep the fear from her voice. She didn't want him to know how scared she'd been. How many times she thought her life could be over at any minute.

Knowing someone wished you were dead was an odd feeling. One that didn't move to the back of your mind easily. It stayed with you, front and center every hour of every day. Especially when you were all that was standing between that person and the little boy that meant more to you than anything in the world.

"You don't have to worry about him anymore." The matter-of-fact way Wade said it made her blink.

"Why?"

"Because I'm going to kill him." Wade sounded like he was simply explaining that the sky was blue.

"You can't just kill someone."

"I can, and I have." The tone in his voice made her think he wasn't kidding.

Wade's whole body went still. Just like the night they met, right before a car almost ended her life.

Would have ended her life if Wade hadn't pulled her to safety in the blink of an eye and shielded her body with his.

Wade stepped back, moving toward the door of the bedroom. "Stay here." The tone of his voice was low and sharp.

Bess gaped at his back as he reached into the waistband of his jeans and pulled out a gun, moving without a sound as he left the room, pulling the door silently closed as he went.

Her heart picked up speed.

Had Chris already found her? Her father said this was the only way to keep them safe. Ship her and her son to an isolated town in the depths of Alaska where they would be guarded round the clock.

Protected by men who would do whatever it took to keep her safe.

And one of them might be the key to ending this whole mess.

Or he could make it all worse.

Parker whined. The kind of sound that said he was considering throwing a fit if he wasn't fed soon. "Shit."

She was going to have to stop using that word or it was going to be her son's favorite.

But how bad would that be considering his father might be a mercenary?

That's what someone who killed people was called, right?

Her son's father was either a kidnapper or a murderer. That was great. Just freaking great.

Parker's complaining amped up a little. She had to feed him or he was going to start wailing, and considering Wade just walked out with his gun pulled, silence was probably an important thing.

Going to the kitchen to make him a bottle wasn't an option. That meant she had to give him something she'd finally narrowed down to only being a bedtime thing.

Bess sat in the glider brought in with the crib, and wrestled the v-neck of her shirt down as Parker wiggled, kicking his feet in anticipation. Before he could latch on she pressed a finger to his cheek. "Be nice."

He was one bite away from being completely cut off, and right now weaning an unwilling child wasn't high on her list of things to add to her plate. Bess tried to focus on rocking as she stared at the door, listening for any sounds that might tell her what was happening on the other side of the door.

Shawn assured her this place was secure when he brought her here. Swore no one would find her, and even if they did, there was no way for them to get inside.

The sound of steps on the other side of the door sent her heart to her throat. The urge to stand and be ready to fight was overwhelming.

But she didn't have to fight anymore, and having that taken out of her hands was comforting and terrifying at the same time.

The door clicked open and Wade stood in the doorway. He was silent for a minute before his deep voice filled the room. "Are you hungry? Shawn brought lunch. Takeout." He moved into the room, eyes never leaving her. "Do you have everything you need?"

Bess couldn't look away from him. From the almost wonder in his eyes as he watched her. "I'm okay."

He shook his head. "You have to need something. Make a list of anything you need and I'll have it brought in tomorrow." Wade stopped just beside her chair and slowly lowered to his knees. "Anything he needs I'll get."

Every day since she saw those damn pink lines on that pregnancy test a month after her night with Wade, Bess had wondered what he would think if he knew.

How he would react to the possibility that he was a father.

She never expected to find out.

"Are you upset?"

"Not with you." Wade stroked the same soft hair she kissed every morning and night. "He has dark hair."

"He does." Bess struggled to breathe. Finding this man was a pipe dream for so long. A means to an end. Proving he was Parker's father and that Chris was not, would mean her ex had no legal footing to fight for visitation.

But now she realized Chris might not be the only man wanting time with Parker. "That doesn't necessarily mean he's yours."

Wade's eyes lifted to hers and the hurt she saw there would have sent her stumbling back if she wasn't seated.

Was it that easy to wound a man who murdered people?

"What color are his eyes?"

The question sat between them. Bess didn't want to answer. This was all happening too fast. She needed time to think. To consider the possibilities.

"Bess." Wade's tone was soft as he leaned in closer, his hand coming to cradle her cheek. "What color are Parker's eyes?"

Tears bit at her lids, born of fear and longing. Fear this man might try to take away the only thing that mattered to her. Longing for a completely different sort of outcome. One she was sure could never be. "They're dark."

It was why she was almost positive Parker belonged to the man she couldn't forget. The nameless stranger who gave her so much more than he realized that night.

Until now.

"Brown?" It was hesitant. Like Wade wanted to hold back. Wait to be sure, before letting himself believe it could be true.

She understood that completely. The minute Chris discovered she was pregnant, he began harassing her, positive the baby was his even though she assured him it wasn't.

And that made everything worse.

Wade slowly leaned to one side, clicking on the lamp sitting on the table at her elbow. Parker squinted, kicking a little at the sudden change. He pulled from her breast and rolled toward the man watching him with the same intensity she remembered.

The sharp intake of breath was almost as unmistakable as the midnight eyes her son had developed over the past few months. Wade leaned closer, black eyes staring into their match.

Parker swung at Wade's face, catching one cheek with a slap before patting it a few times. Wade never flinched. Never even looked close to considering moving away. He kept watching Parker as the baby's attention turned to the hat covering his head, little chubby fingers grabbing at the knit beanie hiding Wade's own dark hair. "You had to take care of him alone."

"Not alone. My friend Cricket was there to help. And my parents." Bess struggled to swallow as Parker finally managed to pull Wade's hat free. His lips lifted immediately as the baby swung the cap in the air between them. It was the first time she'd seen his smile in almost two years, and it was just as devastatingly perfect as she remembered. "I had help."

"Not the kind you needed." The words sounded bitter. For the first time something about him was different. Carried an angry edge she didn't remember.

It was an anger she shared. Not necessarily at him.

Maybe a little.

"You could have found me if you wanted." The knowledge sat cold and heavy in her stomach, souring any happiness she wanted to feel.

Wade was part of a team that hunted people. It was his business to be able to find anyone.

Yet he never tried to find her.

"I told you. I'm not the kind of man you should be with."

All the emotion she felt at seeing him again, the warmth, the gnaw of excitement, it all disappeared in an instant. "I agree."

Maybe it was better this way. Better that she know right up front his stance was still the same.

Better that it was. It meant chances were good he didn't think he was the kind of man Parker should have as a father either. Parker would still be only hers.

And that was perfectly fine.

Wade stared silently at her. "You should." He slowly stood. "Come eat."

"I'm not hungry."

His ebony eyes narrowed on her for a second, assessing. "Fine." He stepped toward the door.

"The food will be in the fridge if you change your mind." He turned to leave.

"Wait." Bess clamped her mouth shut.

Why did she just stop him? She should let him go. Literally.

Wade's head tipped to look at her over one shoulder.

She fumbled through her overwhelmed brain for something to say. "Are you leaving?"

His head barely shook. "No."

"Oh." That was perfectly fine too. She could handle him being here. Hell, she'd dealt with freaking Chris, and he'd tried to kill her. "When do the shifts switch?" Shawn said there would be a team of two men covering her, taking turns unless things got serious.

Hopefully they didn't get serious.

Wade turned back to face her and slowly stalked toward the chair where she sat. "The shifts won't be switching."

"Shawn said—"

Wade leaned down, resting one hand on each of the arms of the glider. "Shawn was wrong."

"But—"

His eyes moved down to level with hers. "No one will be here but me, Sweetheart. You're stuck with me for the foreseeable future." His gaze barely dipped to Parker before coming back to meet hers. "Only me."

His closeness was all it took to make her heart rate pick back up. The familiar scent of birch and earth flooded her mind with memories of that single night they shared. A night that still meant more to her than it probably should.

Because whether she wanted to admit it to herself or not, it was real. In spite of Wade's belief that he was not the man for her, she still wanted him. Still had to fight not to lean closer, hoping he might hold her the way he did when he first came here.

Before he found out about Parker.

The realization added one more layer to the mounting pile of turmoil burying her alive.

Had Wade thought they would share another night like before? That their time here would be filled with cabin coitus until he saw there was a baby to piss all over his passion parade?

Wade dropped to a crouch. "What about you, Buddy? Are you hungry?"

Parker immediately grabbed at Wade, falling into his waiting arms with a giggle and squeal that only got louder when Wade lifted him high in the air as he stood. "How about you come with me so your momma can have a break?"

Bess jumped up from her seat. "You don't have to do that. I—" She reached for Parker and to his credit, Wade didn't try to pull him away.

But he didn't immediately hand him over either. Wade tucked Parker into one arm, cradling him close as the baby bounced in his hold. "We will be right outside the door, Bess." His voice was soft. "There's a Jacuzzi tub in the bathroom. Go. Relax. I'll bring him back in an hour."

"You want to take him for an hour?" A familiar fear bit at her gut. "But what if—"

"Nothing will happen to him, Bess." Wade's free hand came to cradle her cheek. "I swear to you. Parker will always be safe with me."

"Because you'll kill anyone who tries to hurt him?" She pressed her lips together too late, shutting down the question after it had already been asked.

"Yes."

The answer was simple and honest.

Wade would kill anyone who tried to hurt Parker. It should scare her a little that he was more than ready to murder to protect her son.

But it didn't. Not at all.

Because so was she.

CHAPTER 3

WADE WALKED FASTER toward the kitchen, forcing himself not to turn back. He needed a minute away from Bess. Time to get himself together.

It had been almost impossible not to kiss her.

For the first time Wade was seeing the side of Bess he'd suspected was there that first night.

He'd never fallen for anyone as hard and fast as he did Bess and this was the reason.

She'd seen him in a way no one ever had. Been able to see right through the walls most people didn't even try to peek over.

That was also why he had to leave her behind. She was too smart. Too intuitive. Too easy to be with.

Maybe it was because they were so much alike.

It's why he knew the panicked look in her eyes when he told her he wanted to take Parker so she could rest. Loss of control was about the worst thing anyone could do to him.

As long as he was in charge, he knew shit would go right. Because he would make sure it did.

It was a stubborn streak he knew she had, even if it didn't show the night he met her. Now it was on full display. It was there in the way she held herself. The way she refused to be broken by the past year of her life.

The anger he'd been fighting since walking into cabin five threatened to push through. Wade tamped it down, pulling Parker a little closer. "That momma of yours is something else, Buddy."

Parker babbled a little in response, the string of nonsense starting with one, very obvious word. "Ma-ma-ma-ma-ma-mm."

"That's right, Buddy. We've gotta take care of her." Wade grabbed the high-chair beside the long table set between the kitchen and the great room and hauled it to the row of barstools set along the island. It was where he preferred to eat when he was stationed in this cabin. It also made a great make-shift office with plenty of space to spread out.

Which is what he was going to do now.

As soon as he figured out what in the hell babies ate.

Wade looked at the child in his arms. "Are you even still a baby?"

Parker shook his head until he started to fall back. Wade angled him back upright. "Didn't think so." He opened the fridge, hoping Shawn had done at least a little shopping. A stack of yogurt cups with a baby on the front sat on one shelf. "These yours?" He sorted through them, checking the flavors, settling on blueberry. "You like blueberry?"

Parker grabbed the container and started chewing on it as Wade grabbed a spoon from the drawer.

His experience with babies was limited. Greatly.

He'd never held one until today. Until this baby that might be his.

Might. Wade snorted as he worked Parker down into his highchair, getting his first good look at Bessie's son. He was a cute kid. Had his momma's wide eyes and straight nose.

But the rest looked real damn familiar. "I think you might be stuck with me as your dad, Buddy."

Parker didn't look too worried about the idea of having someone like him as his paternal donor.

At least one of them wasn't concerned.

Wade stopped peeling back the foil lid on Parker's yogurt, leaving it half-opened.

Is that all he would be?

A fucking donor?

The thought bothered him on an uncomfortable level, especially considering he'd had no intention of ever fathering a kid. It wouldn't be fair.

It's why he was always so careful, and Wade was absolutely sure he'd been careful that night with Bess.

He never wanted anyone to go through the things his mother went through. Never wanted any kid to live the same kind of life he had.

But here he was. Stuck in a sick cycle of history repeating itself. Getting a woman pregnant and then leaving.

Except he left of his own volition.

His eyes lifted to the room where Bess was probably working hard to handle her son being out of her sight, instead of relaxing like he told her to. Was that all she would want him to be? The guy who knocked her up?

And then left.

"I fucked up, Buddy." Wade went back to the yogurt, opening the container the rest of the way and scooping out a bite for Parker before holding it out to him. "I shouldn't have left your momma."

It was old news. He'd regretted walking away from Bess immediately.

Leaving her sleeping in his hotel room was the hardest thing he'd ever done, but Wade was convinced he had to do it.

And he'd stuck to that belief until about an hour ago.

Now he knew it was as fucking wrong as it felt. Every day it got worse. The memory of her had only gotten stronger with each day that passed.

And Bess was everything he remembered her to be. Better maybe.

Motherhood had rounded her hips and her breasts, adding a little more curve to her small frame. "I probably shouldn't be noticing that, huh?" He held out another bite for Parker. "Those are your territory now."

He let out a sigh as Parker started blowing blueberry-yogurt-laced raspberries and banging his hands on the tray to his high-chair. "What in the hell am I going to do?"

It was an easy answer. As simple as it should have been two years ago.

But back then the execution would have been much easier. At that point he didn't have a crazy ex and two years of unknown abandonment to overcome.

Wade grabbed a towel from the drawer and ran it under warm water before using it to clean up Parker. Taking care of him was a whole lot like taking care of a lot of the people he was hired to protect.

Only this baby was much more agreeable.

Wade was just pulling Parker from the high-chair when the hair on the back of his neck lifted.

Someone was watching the cabin.

He'd done this for enough years that it didn't take eyes on the enemy for him to know they were there. Wade tucked Parker close and crossed to the large armoire in the great room, opening the doors to reveal the bank of small screens hidden in the piece of furniture. He flipped the switch, turning them all on at once. It took him seconds to locate the source of his unease.

Sitting at the end of a service road crossing behind the property was a snowmobile with two riders.

Could be nothing. Someone out for a ride in the fresh snowfall.

Wade watched as the two masked riders stared toward the cabin, their heads moving slightly as they spoke to each other.

Maybe he shouldn't have made Brock leave. If his partner was here he'd be halfway to where the snowmobile sat by now.

"What are you doing?"

Bessie's voice made him jump. He spun to face her.

She shouldn't have been able to sneak up on him like that. "Nothing."

One pale brown brow lifted. "That doesn't look like nothing."

She leaned to peek around him and he stepped along with her, blocking her view of the screens. "I was just making sure all the cameras were working."

Bess narrowed her eyes. "What did you see?"

"Nothing."

"So this is how it's going to be?" She stepped closer, bringing the deep dark scent that owned a place in his brain along with her. "You want to keep lying to each other?"

Wade tried to come up with a response, but was at a loss. "I don't know what to tell you."

"How about the truth?" Her eyes snapped to a spot just over his shoulder and the color drained from her face. "There's someone on the camera."

The fear in her expression sent his adrenaline spiking. If this was anyone else he'd be on the phone with Brock right now, calling for backup.

He couldn't let his desires outweigh what was best for Bess and Parker and that's exactly what he was doing.

It looked like the privacy he wanted to have while sorting this out with Bess would have to wait.

Wade glanced at the spot where Bess was staring. The two riders were off the snow mobile now, creeping through the bank of trees between the service road and the cabin, each taking a different path, both moving like they'd done this before.

"Take Parker and go to the closet in your bedroom." He shoved the little boy into his momma's arms. "Bolt the door and don't unlock it until you hear my voice."

"You're voice?" Her feet didn't move fast enough as he pushed her toward the bedroom.

"It's a safe room with an intercom. Stay in it until I tell you to come out." Wade pushed her harder, needing Bess to get to safety so he could get outside and deal with the pricks fucking up his plans. "Go. Now."

He expected her to buck at the command. Instead she gave him one final look over her shoulder, eyes wide, skin pale, before doing as he asked and rushing into the bedroom. Wade waited for the sound of the lock clicking into place before grabbing his phone and racing to the back of the house. Brock answered on the first ring.

"What the fuck was that all ab—"

"I need you to get here now." Wade pulled on one of the white overcoats and knit masks in the back room. "We've got two in the back."

"Fuck." Brock shuffled on the other end of the line. "You can't go out there without backup, man."

"I can." Wade pulled his gun from his waistband before zipping the coat. "Get here fast." He hung up on Brock and set the phone on the bench beside the door before silently slipping outside.

What he wouldn't give to have Dutch in his ear right now, telling him where the bastards were. Wade moved toward the tree line, staying low, trying to keep as close to the ground as possible. The coat and mask meant his upper body blended in with the snow-covered surroundings, but the jeans covering his lower-half would stand out until he was in the woods. That meant he had to risk moving fast in favor of gaining cover.

The first shot caught him by complete surprise, but the second one he was ready for.

Wade dropped to the ground and rolled against a bank of snow shoveled from the back deck of the house, using it as cover. He was well off to the side of the house, but could still see the back of the building and all the windows that encompassed it. Their reflective surfaces gave him a full view of the woods. Wade held his breath. Waiting.

They couldn't stay hidden forever, and soon the two men who were enjoying their last minutes of life would make a move.

And he would end them.

Killing was usually a last resort. One even Team Rogue tried to avoid under normal circumstances.

But these circumstances were anything but normal.

Nothing shifted in the shadowed scene on the glass. Not so much as a whisper carried on the air around him. Everything was silent. Still.

Until it wasn't.

Tires crunched hard and fast up the icy driveway to cabin five a second before doors opened and boots pounded the frozen ground, racing through the snow as they surrounded the house and spread through the woods. Almost a dozen men raced over the property, their white gear making them blend in as they ran, guns drawn.

The biggest of the group came straight toward Wade at a full sprint, barrel trained right between his eyes.

Wade didn't even flinch. He wouldn't give the ass the satisfaction.

"What the fuck are you doing?" Brock flipped up the knit mask covering his face. "You pull some shit like that again I'll kill you myself."

"I got something." Nate's voice carried from deep in the trees.

Brock glanced toward the woods. "Be right there." He shoved one hand Wade's way. "Get your ass up."

Wade took his partner's hand and let Brock heft him up from the snow. "I couldn't just let them get away."

"That's what you fucking did, though. If you waited we could have been here and taken them down as a team, dick." Brock led him toward where Nate stood at the access road they sometimes used to smuggle people in and out of cabin five.

Nate was in a crouch, taking pictures of a set of tracks with his phone. "These are big. Probably both men." He stood, placing one of his own boots next to one of the prints in the snow before taking another picture. "You get that?"

Wade glared at Brock until his friend pulled out his own earpiece and handed it over, yanking it back just as Wade reached for it. "I expect to know what the fuck's going on."

"Fine." He snatched the lifeline away and shoved it into his ear. "Dutch, it's Wade. What do you have?"

Dutch was the team's tech guy. He was everywhere and nowhere. All from the comfort of his office at headquarters. He watched all their cameras, listened to all their lines, and dished out intel while sucking down espresso and shining his fucking shoes.

"What the actual fuck, Wade?"

"Come here and say that to my face." Wade carefully stepped around the tracks in the snow, studying the familiar-looking tread pattern.

"One day I'll kick your ass just to prove I can so you'll shut the fuck up about it." Dutch made a loud sipping noise on the other end of the line in Wade's ear. "I bet it's fucking cold out there after being on the beach, isn't it?"

"Fuck off." Wade tipped his head to one side as he continued staring at the print. "You lookin' at the shots Nate sent?"

"Of course I'm fucking looking at the shots Nate sent. You think I just sit around drinking hot coffee while you freeze your ass off?"

"That's exactly what I think." Wade tipped the boot he was wearing to one side, comparing the pattern to the one punched in the snow. "It looks familiar."

"That's because it's from a tactical boot." The sound of Dutch's fingers flying over one of the keyboards in his office carried into Wade's ear. "Hate to be the bearer of bad news, but those weren't just some dudes taking their new sled out for a ride."

"Wade!" Abe stood on the deck leading to the main part of cabin five, his arms lifted in the air. "Your girl won't come out of the fucking closet."

Your girl.

It was a term he'd never heard directed his way before. It didn't sound as foreign as he would have expected. "I'm coming."

He pulled the piece from his ear and handed it back to Brock. "Tell Dutch I'll get with him."

The warm air of the cabin was more welcome than he cared to admit. Now was not the time for him to go soft on the cold. He had to be at the top of his game for Bess, and already he'd shown she made him anything but.

Abe was standing at the speaker outside the closet when Wade walked into the room. "I swear he's here. You can come out."

"No." Bessie's answer was short and sharp.

Abe shot him a look over one shoulder as he released the button on the intercom. "Don't look so happy. You need to talk to her. She has to listen to all of us. Not just your smug ass."

"I told her she could only come out when I said it was safe." His finger hovered over the button.

"That's not what will keep her safe and you know it." Abe stared him down. "I don't know who she is to you, but she will be safer if we can all protect her. Not just you."

Brock and his big fucking mouth. "I'll take that under advisement." Wade punched the button just as Brock walked into the bedroom with Nate on his heels. "Bess."

There was no answer for a minute. Finally the sound of an open line came over the speaker.

"Who's Abe?"

Wade glanced at the man beside him.

Every fiber of his being wanted to be the one to keep Bess and Parker safe.

To be their protector.

But Abe was right. "He's one of the guys I work with."

"How many guys do you *work with*?" The way she said it made him pause. He'd admitted more to Bess in the past hour than even his own mother knew about what he did for a living. "On my team there are ten of us."

"Your team?"

He held the button with more force. "Come out and we can talk about this."

"No."

"No?"

"No."

Wade stared at the speaker for a second. "How the fuck do I make her come out?"

Abe shook his head. "Got me man." He lifted one shoulder. "Maybe offer to take her shopping?"

Wade shook his head. "This woman isn't like the normal type we deal with."

The offer of a shopping trip would only piss Bess off. If he was right all those nights ago about who she was, then there was only one way he could get her out of that room right now. Wade stepped closer, hovering right in front of the speaker box as he pressed the button, hopefully for the last time. "The men on the sled were here for you, Bess. I don't know who they are yet, but I will. And when I know, you will be the first person I tell."

Wade released the button and waited.

"Why in the hell did you tell her that?" Brock stepped closer. "You're going to scare the shit out of her."

Wade shook his head. "Not her."

A second later the bolt keeping him from her clicked open. He immediately pushed the door open and caught Bess as she fell into him. "Shawn said he wouldn't be able to find us."

Wade pulled her close, pressing his face into her hair as he held her and Parker in his arms. "I know, Sweetheart."

She rested her forehead against his chest and barely sniffed. "I'm so freaking tired of this." Bess took a deep breath and stepped out of his embrace too soon. Her chin lifted and she looked into his eyes, her gaze was steady and solid, burning with an inner strength he'd have to be blind not to see. "I'm fine."

Wade nodded, easing back, even though all he wanted was to pull her and Parker close again.

The second he moved, Brock took a step forward, one hand out. "I'm Bro- holy shit." His eyes locked onto the baby in Bessie's arms for a second. His brows slowly came together. "Wade?"

He shot Brock a glare. "Shut it."

CHAPTER 4

BESS LOOKED FROM Wade to the man beside him. "What did you say your name was?"

The other man seemed to recover from his shock, shoving his dark hair back with one hand while reaching the other out to her once again. "Brock. I'm this asshole's partner."

"You can't say shit like that, man." The man who must be Abe, based on his unmistakably deep voice, nodded to Parker. "She's got a baby."

Brock pointed at Abe. "You just said shit."

"Shit." Abe's eyes darted to Parker. "Sorry, baby."

"His name's Parker." Wade eased a little closer to her side. "And he's not a baby."

"What would you call him then?" Brock lifted his brows at Wade who looked to Bess.

"He's a toddler."

Wade nodded once. "Toddler." His attention turned back to Bess. "Does that mean he can walk?"

The question was softer than the words that came before it.

Bess nodded. "He started walking when he was ten months old."

"Ten months." Wade's eyes trained on Parker as he started grabbing at the heavy canvas of the white coat he was wearing. "What else has he already done?"

The question made her chest ache a little. "He's done lots of things."

And Wade missed all of them.

She'd always imagined finding the man she believed fathered her son, and every time he was ecstatic. Thrilled to find her, and beside himself over being a dad. But that was a fantasy. One she never in a million years thought would turn into reality.

And it hadn't.

Right now Wade seemed anything but happy. The line of his lips was tight and thin as he straightened. "We have to go over some things. Are you okay on your own while I talk with the team?"

Bess stood tall. "I want to come too." If it involved her son's safety then she intended to be front and center.

Wade glanced at the other three men in the room. "Give us a minute."

Without a word they left, pulling the door closed behind them. Wade waited until the knob clicked into place before turning to her, his eyes serious. "If you're there they won't be honest. They will hold back on the truth because they'll expect it to upset you."

"It won't."

"I know that, but they don't, Sweetheart." Wade moved in closer until the thick barrier of his coat brushed the arms holding her son. "I will tell you everything, but you can't be there. Not right now."

She was stuck. Left at the mercy of a group of men she didn't know, forced to go along with what they deemed best and safest.

She'd seen how that went.

"They said we would be safe here." The relief she initially felt being in Alaska was gone. For the first time since this all started Bess thought it was all going to be okay. That there would finally be something stronger than her standing between Parker and the man she never should have given so much of her time. "They said he wouldn't find us."

It was why she agreed to come here. Because it seemed like it should be true. There's no way Chris should have been able to find her here. It was freaking Alaska for God's sake.

Wade's hands came up to cradle her face. "They were right, Bess. You are safe here."

She swallowed hard as all the feelings she carried for the past two years threatened to show themselves. How could she feel so much for a man she'd spent less than twenty-four hours with?

"He might find you, but he will never hurt you. Not ever again." The last word was harsh. Angry.

"I didn't know he was like this."

"That's not a good sign, Sweetheart." Wade held her as she tried to step away, his hands on her face firm, but still so very gentle. "If you didn't know he was like this then he's crazy as hell." His thumbs stroked over her cheeks. "If he fooled you then he can fool anyone." Wade's gaze shifted to one side for just a minute before coming back to hers. His big body eased in a little more, getting as close as was possible with a baby in the middle of them. Parker's head dropped to her chest. He'd been getting heavier over the course of the conversation and would be asleep any second.

"I should put him down for a nap."

Wade's hands slowly eased away. "His momma should take a nap too." He leaned in to press a kiss to her forehead. "There's eyes all over this place. No one will get close again." He backed away. "If you need me, I'll be in the office."

When he was gone she crossed to the window and used one finger to peek out the blinds. The long driveway was filled with black SUVs that looked identical to the one that picked her up from the airport and brought her here.

Her father told her the company he hired was the best there was, but this was so much more than she expected.

And Chris still found her.

Or someone Chris hired. There were two men on that snowmobile lurking at the back of the cabin, and unless they were looking for whoever Wade's company holed up here before her, then that only meant one thing.

Even the best around might not be able to keep Parker safe.

Bess let the blind fall into place and went to the giant king-sized bed that barely made a dent in the footprint of the room. She carefully laid her sleeping son in the center of the mattress, propping a pillow behind his back before crawling on the bed beside him and curling around his tiny body.

She was so tired. Tired of worrying. Tired of always having to be careful. Tired of the fear that ruled her life.

But whether he wanted her or not, Wade seemed ready and willing to take that burden on. God knows he was big enough to carry it.

And maybe she should let him.

Just for a little while.

****

"BESSIE, SWEETHEART."

Her eyes flew open and she sat straight up, blinking at the unexpected darkness of the room. "What's wrong?"

"Nothing. Everything is fine." Wade's voice was calm but her heart was still racing.

She reached out for Parker. The second her hand met empty space Bess was off the bed and racing to the door. "He's gone. Parker's gone again."

Wade was on her in a second, grabbing her from behind, pulling her back against the width of his chest. "Parker is okay. He's with Brock in the kitchen." His hold on her tightened. "What do you mean, again?"

Bess let out the air trapped in her lungs. Parker was safe.

"Chris took him." Her chin threatened to shake at the memory. The absolute helplessness she felt knowing her baby was with a monster. It was the last time she trusted anyone else to take care of Parker. In the blink of an eye he was gone. "Threatened to kill me if I came after him."

"What did you do?" His tone was eerily calm. Like they were talking about the weather.

"I went after him." Her fingers found the spot on her arm, sliding over the smooth scars she earned that day.

Wade was silent behind her. Strong and solid at her back.

How many times could she have used his presence? Would it have kept Chris from doing the things he did?

Maybe. Maybe not.

"Not many people would do something like that. You're very brave."

Bess nodded. It was all she could manage. All she trusted herself to do. Breaking down was never an option. Parker needed her to be strong. To be what Wade called her.

Brave.

"I meant what I said earlier, Bess. I won't stop until he's dead." Wade's voice was cold. An icy promise that did nothing but warm her inside.

Because she would do the same if the opportunity presented itself. "Killing someone is illegal."

It was the only thing that kept her from doing unthinkable acts. Knowing her son would have to grow up without her.

"That's one way to look at it." Wade's arms relaxed a little.

Bess turned her head to look at him over one shoulder. "Is there another way?"

His eyes were unwavering as they held hers. "The world is just better off without some people."

"Chris is one of those people." She was one of the only ones who knew it until the day he took Parker. Bess tried to tell anyone who would listen. Her attorney. The advocate assigned to her case. She told them all he was spiraling into someone she didn't recognize. None of them listened.

Probably because Wade was right. Chris was a master of manipulation. He'd managed to do it to her for years, and only when she finally walked away did he let the beast loose, and it had been breathing down her neck ever since.

"Not for long." Wade's hand covered hers, easing her fingers from the spot that would never let her forget that day. His touch was feather light as it smoothed over her scarred skin, finding each jagged edge of the slice Chris gave her for daring to take back her baby.

"He's a senator's son."

"Doesn't matter."

Bess spun to face him. "Bullshit." Anger flared, hot and ready. "It's why he's free now. Even after everything he's done, he is out there, walking around while I can't leave the house without looking over my shoulder every second, worried he's going to try to finish what he started."

"He's going to try. That's why you're here." Wade's words were too calm. Too relaxed.

"So I just have to sit here and wait for him to come get me? For him to take Parker from me again?"

Wade shook his head. "I said try, Sweetheart. He won't touch you again." His hands skimmed up her arms. "Not ever." He caught a few strands of her hair, dark eyes watching as it slipped through his fingers. "And he won't so much as set eyes on Parker. I can promise you that."

"Wade?"

Wade didn't turn toward the voice coming from the doorway. "What do you need?"

"I think little man crapped his pants, and that's above my pay grade."

Wade's eyes skimmed over her face one more time before he stepped away to where Brock stood with Parker in his arms. Parker watched Wade with an unusual amount of intensity, waiting until the large man was within arm's reach before giving him a grin, showing off his eight perfect teeth.

Brock passed Parker off, glancing Bessie's way. "He's a cute kid."

"Thank you." Her arms felt restless waiting for Wade to bring Parker to her. She'd kept him close for so long it felt empty without him in her arms. Parker's smile widened as Wade lifted him into a prone position and flew him like an airplane into her waiting embrace. By the time he reached her, Parker was belly laughing so hard his giggles were barely audible. Bess caught him and held him close, resting her nose on his head and breathing deep.

Wade was right beside her in an instant. "I swear to you, Bess. No one will get close to Parker again."

It sounded great.

And she wanted to believe it more than anything, but she'd seen firsthand the lengths Chris was willing to go to in the name of punishing her.

That's what this was really about. Not Parker. Not his desire to have a son he believed was his.

This was all about her. Chris had never been told no in his life. She was the first to deny him anything.

"He doesn't really care about Parker." The admission was almost painful to make. She'd never said it out loud. Not to anyone.

Because it meant she was the one who brought this on her son.

Wade's jaw ticked. "Clearly." He leaned in closer, one hand coming to rest on her back, the other on Parker's, adding a strange feeling of safety with just a touch. "Men who care about their kids respect their mother, whether she wants to be with them or not."

Bess rubbed her lips together to cover the tremble of her chin. "This is my fault."

"You know damn well it's not."

In theory, yes. She knew the fault here all rested on one person. That didn't make it feel true. "It's easy to say, but—"

"If you really believe this is your fault, then ultimately it makes it my fault." Wade stepped away, taking the safety his presence brought with him. "If it wasn't for me, he wouldn't have Parker to use against you." He started to say something else but stopped, barely shaking his head before continuing. "Change Parker and come eat something."

For some reason his desire to take all the blame in the situation didn't sit well. "You're being bossy."

"I am bossy." He pointed to the stack of diapers sitting on the dresser. "Do it."

She barely had the scoff all the way out before he was gone, leaving her staring after him.

Parker bounced a little in her arms, sending a whiff of dirty-diaper stink into the air.

"Ugh." Bess let out a loud sigh as she made her way across the thick-piled carpet of the giant room. "He's a pain in the a—" She eyed her son. "Butt."

She was just finishing up the diaper change when soft steps padded into the room behind her. Bess spun, ready to tell Wade she would eat when she was damn well ready.

Brock stopped walking, his dark brows lifting. "I hope that look's not for me."

"What look? There is no look." Bess popped her hip, resting her son's freshly-diapered butt against it.

"There's definitely a look." Brock grinned. "I fuckin' love it." His dark eyes widened, bouncing to Parker before coming back to her. "I meant freakin'."

Bess waited for him to go on. Instead Brock just kept grinning at her. "What do you need?"

"I'm supposed to make sure you eat something." Brock took a step back. "I'm willing to lure you to the kitchen with an inordinate amount of charm and flattery."

"I'm not that kind of girl."

"That takes away about half of my arsenal then." Brock barely turned his head to one side. "Are you a chocolate cake sort of girl?"

Bess hoped he was far enough away to miss the rumble of her stomach. It had been forever since she'd been able to enjoy food. The constant fear she'd lived with went straight to her belly, making it almost impossible to finish a meal before the urge to throw up came. "You think you can bribe me with cake?"

Brock shook his head. "Not me."

Wade.

It would figure he'd somehow magically know her affinity for cake. The man had miraculously been able to check off boxes she didn't know existed from the very beginning. "Where is Wade?"

"Not scared to come back in here if that's what you're asking." Brock gave her a wink. "At least that's what he claims." Wade's partner backed toward the door. "He's on a call with Shawn and Dutch. They're trying to figure out who came by for a visit."

Bess started to follow him, the thought of cake propelling her on. "Why are you telling me this?"

Wade said his team would hold back if she was there, worried the truth would scare her. Obviously they didn't know how much it took to scare her these days.

"Wade said I should tell you anything you wanted to know."

"Did he?" Bess took a step toward the door, this time moving for more than chocolate cake. "Where is Wade now?"

"In the office. You wanna go?" Brock's grin was back.

"I do."

Brock nodded toward the great room outside the door. "Come on."

Bess followed him into the great room which now smelled much different than before she fell asleep. "You *baked* a cake?" She'd assumed the cake Brock offered was brought in from the store, but the telltale scent of freshly-baked chocolate made it seem otherwise.

"Not me darlin'." He barely knocked on one of the closed doors on the other side of the house before opening it and standing aside. "He's all yours."

Bess stepped in, forcing herself not to hesitate. Wade's eyes were on her the second she cleared the doorway. He stood from the chair he'd been sitting in, cell pressed to his ear as he nodded to a set of armchairs beside a large window. "Where do the tracks stop at?"

She sat in one of the chairs as Wade came to the one next to it, dragging it closer to hers before sitting down.

"Someone picked them up then." He reached for a Rubik's cube sitting on the table beside him and passed it to Parker as he leaned back in his chair, resting one hand on her son's back as his eyes stayed on hers. "That's true."

He listened for a few more minutes, occasionally offering a few words in agreement, before hanging up.

Wade's eyes moved over her face for a minute. Finally he took a long breath and leaned in.

"We need to talk."

CHAPTER 5

THAT DIDN'T SOUND good.

"About?"

"Chris filed an emergency injunction."

Her temporary reprieve from the nausea ruling her stomach was over. Bess swallowed down the urge to gag. "What does that mean?"

"It means he's claiming you illegally took his child out of state."

"He's not on Parker's birth certificate. He has no legal claim to him. None." It was the one leg she had to stand on this whole time.

"He's also trying to force the paternity test."

Her belly squeezed the way it always did at those two words, threatening to empty her stomach of the nothing inside it. "He can't do that. They already denied him."

"He can contest the decision. You know that." Wade scooted to the edge of his chair and rested his hands on her knees. "You can beat him to the punch." His eyes fell to the little boy between them. "I can have someone here in the morning. We can have the results in twenty-four hours."

"They take longer than that." She'd looked into it. Checked to see exactly how many days she would have to disappear if Chris was ever successful with his bid to have his DNA tested against Parker's.

Wade's lips barely lifted in a smile. "Maybe for most people."

In less than two days she could know, beyond a shadow of a doubt, who Parker's father was. "What if it's him?"

Wade stood up and reached one hand out to her. "If I didn't already know who Parker belonged to I wouldn't be doing the test, Sweetheart. This is just a formality."

"It won't help anything." She struggled to swallow. "It might even make things worse."

Wade's smile lifted a little more. "I'm counting on that." He stepped closer, reaching for her with his outstretched hand. "Come on. It's time to eat."

Bess leaned deeper into her seat as her stomach started to roll. "I'm not hungry."

Wade rested both hands on the arms of her chair and leaned down until they were eye-level for the second time today. "I don't care." His gaze barely skimmed down her body. "You haven't been taking care of yourself and I'm not having it."

"You're not having it?" She reached out and poked one finger right in the center of his chest. A chest she'd seen up close and personal.

Naked.

She poked it again, the memory of the tiny sprinkling of dark hair hiding beneath her finger sidetracking her brain.

"Something wrong, Sweetheart?"

Her eyes jumped up to his, only to find Wade's smile was back and bigger than ever. "No."

Bess pushed him out of the way as she jumped up from her seat, hauling Parker along as she went. Before she could get anywhere, Wade snagged her and spun her around, catching her and Parker gently against his chest. "Don't pretend what we had isn't still there." He reached up to smooth the spot between her eyebrows with the pad of his thumb. Wade's fingers grazed the side of her face, trailing down her cheek until his warm palm cupped the line of her jaw. "Because you know damn well it is."

There was a light rap on the office door a second before it clicked open. "What'd you find—"

"Get out." Wade didn't turn toward Brock as he ordered him from the room.

"Sorry."

Bess barely heard the mumbled apology because Wade was creeping closer, a familiar intensity burning in his eyes. "You didn't have to yell at him."

"I'll apologize later if you want me to."

She eyed him. "You would do it if I told you to?"

"Still the same as it was two years ago, Sweetheart. I'm in control, but you're in charge."

The night they met had been one of the best, most unique encounters of her life. Not just because it was the only one-night stand she'd ever had.

From the first word, Wade proved to be very different from most men she knew. Most people she knew.

And he seemed to feel the same about her.

Bess straightened under his heated gaze. "It's not still the same as two years ago, though. I'm different now."

The past two years had been the most difficult she'd ever experienced, not that it was a challenge to earn that spot. She'd lived a charmed life, growing up in an affluent, but hard-working family. She went to college and had a job waiting for her in the family business when it was over. Everything was fine until that night.

Then she realized how not fine it actually was, and it all started with this man.

"I hated you for leaving me."

"So did I." Wade paused. "I had to talk myself out of finding you every goddamn day."

"Why?"

"Why did I talk myself out of it, or why did I want to come find you?"

"Both."

"This." One finger moved between them. "What we have is different. I knew it after one night."

Her breath barely caught. "Why didn't you come for me then?"

His laugh was low and bitter. "Because I thought I would put you in danger."

"I did a pretty good job of that all by myself."

The sourness in his chuckle lifted, leaving behind only a genuine laugh. "You sure did." Wade pulled her closer. "I'm impressed."

"You should be." Bess smiled, unable to carry the weight of her current situation while he was grinning down at her. "I'm not sure you could have done a better job."

"I might have to agree with you." Wade ran his thumb over her lower lip. "I guess that means I wasted a hell of a lot of time then."

Bess willed herself not to lick the lip he was stroking with maddening softness. When Wade leaned closer her breath caught in her lungs.

"I think I'm done wasting time, Sweetheart."

"Oh?" It was all she could manage to squeak out as Wade's lips hovered over hers.

"Parker is mine." His midnight eyes moved over her face. "And so are you."

And then his lips were there, warm and soft. Firm but careful.

She'd kissed him before and remembered the act in embarrassingly graphic detail.

Or so she thought.

This was not at all what she remembered. One of Wade's hands tangled in her hair, holding her close as he brushed the sweetest kiss over her mouth.

While Parker held the pointer finger of his free hand in one little fist.

LOSS RECOVERY

Wade only kissed her for what felt like the blink of an eye before resting his forehead against hers. "Are you hungry yet?"

Bess swallowed, waiting for the nausea that plagued her to rear its ugly head. It didn't.

Instead her temperamental belly growled loud enough Wade's eyes dropped and the corner of the mouth that was just on hers lifted.

She smiled. "I think I am."

****

BESS STARTED WITH the cake.

After two big pieces she switched to the veggie tray. Now Bess was on to the lasagna and finally slowing down.

Parker was enjoying his dinner almost as much as his momma and had tomato sauce everywhere. It was in his hair, covering his face, behind his ears.

Probably *in* his ears.

Wade wiped down the tray of the high-chair as Parker started to yawn. "I know you're tired, Buddy, but you've gotta have a good wash down before bed." As Wade pulled him from the chair bits of pasta and cheese fell to the floor around him. Bess started to crouch down, napkin in hand, but Brock cut her off, beating her to it with a rag from the sink.

"I got it." He cleaned up the mess before going to rinse the dish rag out. He eyed Wade over one shoulder. "I heard a storm's on its way through."

"Yeah?" Wade was working down the zipper of Parker's sleeper. Attempting to anyway. Somehow the kid had food inside his jammies and it was falling to the floor Brock just cleaned. "How bad?"

He hadn't checked the weather. It was one of the things he planned to do while settling in today.

That was when he thought this would be just another job. Back before he knew his whole life was about to finish the change it started two years ago.

"Bad enough they're warning people about it."

Most places that didn't mean much. Hell, in Texas they warned people when there was going to be two snowflakes.

In Alaska people were used to extreme weather. Not much fazed anyone here.

"What's it bringing in?"

"Supposed to be twenty inches in two hours."

Wade let out a low whistle. "That's a lotta snow at once." He glanced down at Parker's tomato-stained face. "Probably aren't going to be many people getting out tomorrow then, huh?"

"I would say that's a good assumption." Brock winked at Bess. A move he knew damn well would piss Wade off. "Looks like you're stuck with me for a while."

Bess gave him a dazzling smile that only irritated Wade more.

She hadn't given him a smile like that yet, and he was the father of her baby.

"I don't mind." She forked in another bite of lasagna before dropping her napkin over the bits of cheese and sauce remaining. "I don't think I can eat anymore."

Brock grabbed her plate. "You like biscuits and gravy?" His eyes skimmed to Wade, holding for just a second with a gleam of meanness before going back to Bess. "I've heard my sausage gravy is the best."

He might have to kick his best friend's ass. "Considering how many women you cook breakfast for I would imagine you hear that quite often."

The jab didn't seem to bother Brock. He shrugged. "One of us has to make sure the female population feels loved, and you weren't pulling your weight for the past couple of years."

Bess went still, her hazel eyes staying low as she worried her lower lip between her teeth.

Wade glared at Brock over the island separating them. Bess had too much going on right now to add Brock's fucking meddling to the mix.

"I think I'm tired." She pushed her stool away from the granite counter and slid off the seat. She was two steps away before she turned to Brock. "Thank you for dinner." Her eyes didn't lift to him as she stopped to take Parker from his arms. "And thank you for the cake."

Wade watched as she slipped into the master bedroom and closed the door. It was barely latched before he turned to Brock. "What the fuck was that?"

Brock lifted his hands, eyes wide. "I was just trying to help you out, man."

"Don't." Wade grabbed the bag holding his laptop from the floor beside the island. "She had enough to worry about without you making her think I've been fucking pining over her for the past two years."

"You have." Brock snorted. "Not that you told me what your goddamned problem was. I could have helped you find her."

"That's exactly why I didn't tell you." Wade stepped closer. "You think I didn't want to go find her every damn day? See if it was as real as I thought?"

"Then why in the hell didn't you?"

Wade blew out a huff of frustration. "Because I thought I was bad for her. That she would get hurt because of me."

Brock's eyes locked onto his. "She did."

And there it was.

The real truth of the past two years.

If he'd stayed Bess would have been safe. Parker would have had a father.

And fucking Chris Snyder would be rotting in a hole.

Brock shoveled out a chunk of the chocolate cake Wade made while Bess and Parker napped. "Good thing the universe gave your ass a do-over."

"I don't know that it did." Wade glanced back at the closed door standing between him and not one, but two people who he let down. When he kissed her earlier she'd seemed surprised.

Unprepared.

"Only one way to find out." Brock shoved in a huge bite of cake and nodded to the door. "Go ask her."

Wade set his bag down on the ground, the desire to do the paperwork he should dwindling with each passing second.

Asking Bess what she wanted was out of the question, considering the only additional information she had about him was his propensity to make people dead. Add on the fact that he abandoned her and their unborn child, and Wade wasn't willing to gamble on the odds.

He had to show Bess there was more to him. That he could keep her and Parker safe.

Take care of them.

The only issue with that plan was that Wade wasn't sure two of those things were true. He could sure as hell keep them safe.

But was there more to him?

Debatable.

"Stop being a pussy." Brock had the first piece of cake down and was cutting a second.

"Stop putting your nose in my business." Wade pointed to the remaining cake. "And leave some of that for Bess. She needs to eat."

Brock dropped the plastic lid onto the cake pan. "The rest is hers." He backed from the counter. "I'm taking the nice room upstairs since you won't be needing one for long."

Wade didn't have the desire to argue with him. Brock was feeling way more optimistic than he was about the situation. Bess might be willing to forgive his desertion, but it didn't mean she was willing to consider letting him be a part of her life once this was all over.

Not yet.

Wade walked to the master door and stopped, uncertain what he should do next.

Maybe it was best he leave her alone for the rest of the night. Let Bess get her head around all that happened today.

All it could mean.

"You can come in."

Her voice was soft on the other side of the door. It was barely more than a whisper but Wade felt the quiet words as if her lips were against his ear.

He slowly opened the door but didn't step inside. Bess sat on the giant bed. Parker was in a fresh sleeper and tucked into his mother's arms, nursing.

It was suddenly hard to breathe.

Wade pressed one palm to his chest, rubbing away the strange tightness smothering out the air. "I just wanted to see if you needed anything before I went to bed."

Bess carefully slid off the mattress and crossed to the portable crib. She gently placed Parker inside, righting her shirt as she turned back to face him, the fingers of one hand worrying the nails of the other. "Can I ask you something?"

"You can ask me anything."

71

She licked her lips and he fought not to stare at their fullness. Remember the way they felt under his.

"Was he telling the truth?"

Wade's mind stumbled over the memory of the sweet kiss they shared earlier. "Who?"

"Brock." Bess took a few steps toward him. "Was he telling the truth?" She took a quick breath. "About you not..."

Wade waited, watching as she continued to move closer.

Bess stopped a few feet away. "About you and women."

Wade nodded. It was as much of an answer as he wanted to give her. The whole truth of how much that one night affected him was something he didn't completely understand himself. Most of the time he was sure it wasn't all he remembered.

That she wasn't what he really thought. That time and distance gave his mind room to embellish, perfect what was nothing more than a night of good sex.

But it was more. He knew it in a way that defied logic.

"Why?" Her question caught him off-guard.

Wade stepped into the room, closing the last few feet remaining between them. He didn't want to explain. Couldn't really. Not yet.

He reached for her, slow enough she could stop him if she wanted. She didn't.

He cradled her face with one hand. "I thought you couldn't be as beautiful as I remembered." Wade eased closer. "But you are. Maybe even more." He let his thumb slide over her lower lip. The same one she chewed earlier when Brock gave her more information than he should have.

Bessie's eyes settled on his. "You thought of me?"

He shouldn't tell her, but keeping his mouth shut around this woman wasn't any easier now than it was two years ago.

"Every damn day."

CHAPTER 6

"I THOUGHT OF you every fucking second, Bess." Wade's arm wrapped around her waist, pulling Bess close as his eyes shut and his forehead dropped to hers. "I tried to stop but I couldn't no matter what I did."

"I tried to find you." The admission was out before she could even consider stopping it.

Wade's eyes flew open and his head lifted. "Shit."

She let her hands smooth over the front of his shirt, doing her best not to be distracted by the tight ripple of muscle hiding beneath the thermal fabric. He was holding her, so it was only fair that she could touch him too, right? "When I found out I was pregnant." She lifted one shoulder. "But I didn't know your real name so—"

"Bess, I'm so fucking sorry. If I'd known I would have…"

"You would have what?" Her breath caught as she waited for his answer.

She'd imagined it thousands of times. Wondered what might have happened if he hadn't left town that night.

How her life might have been different if he'd stayed.

Wade was quiet for too long, leaving her hanging on every breath he took. Finally he cleared his throat.

"I would have made sure you didn't have to worry about Chris."

"Oh." The answer deflated her a little which was ridiculous. They'd only spent one night together. How she could continue think it would ever be more than that was beyond explanation.

"Bess." Wade's deep voice halted the spiral of doubts starting to pull her under.

She lifted her eyes to meet his. He still held her close, one hand warm on her back, the other curled around her head.

No man had ever held her the way he did.

But he was a killer. A man who used ultimate force to do what had to be done.

And yet he held her so carefully.

"What?"

"Did you only try to find me because of Parker?" The uncertainty in his tone surprised her.

It made her give him the truth, even though she probably shouldn't. "No."

Wade instantly rewarded her bit of honesty, pulling her body flush against his. "Would you have tried to find me if you weren't pregnant?"

The smell of him surrounded her, the earthy scent of wood and man pulling out more tidbits of truth. "Yes."

The growl that rumbled through his chest made her breath catch. "Good." His nose ran alongside hers. "Can I kiss you, Bess?"

"Why are you asking me?"

"Because I don't want to make assumptions just yet."

"But you kissed me earlier."

"That was different." His lips hovered over hers. So close but still out of reach.

"How?"

"That was just a kiss."

She struggled to keep breathing as his fingers worked into her hair. "And this won't be just a kiss?"

Wade shook his head, the lips he was keeping from her barely lifting at the edges. "Definitely not."

"What will it be?" She couldn't make the words much more than a whisper as anticipation tightened her whole body.

Wade's mouth curved into a smile. "Not what you're thinking. Not yet."

Yet.

Bess stood a little straighter. "How do you know what I'm thinking?"

It didn't seem fair that he saw right through her but she wasn't getting the same access.

One finger skimmed down the front of her throat, moving slow and deliberate as it trailed between her breasts. "You're not doing a very good job of hiding it."

She scoffed. "That's not true."

"It is." Wade shifted and a second later her feet were off the floor. "But I'm happy to even the playing field if it makes you feel better."

Bess locked her legs at his waist as her hands gripped his shoulders, scrambling for purchase. Wade's arm at her waist pulled her snug against him. Close enough there was no ignoring his obvious erection.

"Oh." She looked down between their bodies as Wade walked toward the bed.

"Oh?" His grip tightened as he crawled onto the mattress, dragging her body to the center of the giant bed. "What does, *oh* mean?"

"It means I wasn't expecting that."

Wade eased her back onto the pile of pillows. "You weren't expecting me to be constantly hard around you?"

"Constantly?"

He hovered over her. "Constantly."

"That sounds painful."

Wade shrugged. "It's fine. I'm a big boy." He eased his long body down onto hers, bracing most of his weight on his forearms and knees. "You never answered me."

Bess was having a hard time following the conversation. "What?"

"I asked if I could kiss you, and you haven't answered me yet."

"You said it wouldn't be just a kiss." Bess pressed her hands to the blankets beneath her, trying to keep her brain focused. "What else would be involved?"

Two years ago things were very different. She was very different.

Physically as well as mentally.

Two years ago she was in a place where she wanted to take a chance. Pretend she was different just for a night, and do something without analyzing every bit of it and caving under the potential consequences.

That wasn't an option now.

But it didn't count as a chance if she'd already slept with him once, right?

Wade brushed the tip of his nose across the tip of hers. "You're in charge, Sweetheart. Anything else is up to you."

Bess opened her mouth but Wade cut her off.

"But, none of my clothes are coming off tonight."

"That hardly seems fair."

"I don't remember saying I was going to play fair." He smiled. "And you still haven't said I can kiss you, so I'm starting to worry your clothes aren't going to come off either."

"I don't look the same." The admission jumped right out. Like she didn't have the desire to hide her insecurity, which she definitely did.

"I know." Wade's voice was lower now, rougher. "I didn't think you could get anymore perfect, but I believe I was wrong."

He obviously wasn't understanding what she was saying. "I had a baby."

"And?" Wade's lips moved from their spot just over hers to press against the skin of her neck. He growled again, low and deep. "God you taste just like I remembered." His tongue slid over her flesh. "So fucking sweet."

Her desire to prepare him for the difference in her physique was waning, but she had to be strong, otherwise the sight of her marred skin might shock the crap out of him. "I have stretch marks." Her breath hitched as he found the spot just below her ear. "And my," Bess tried to motion to her breasts but Wade's big body covered them, "my chest is different."

"Oh, I noticed that already." Wade sucked the lobe of her ear between his teeth before scraping it free. "Like I said, you somehow managed to improve on perfection."

Bess heaved out a loud sigh of frustration. Fine. She was just going to lay it all out for him. "Wade, I'm trying to tell you I don't look good naked. My stomach is all soft and stretch-marked, and my nipples are—"

His mouth covered hers, cutting off her explanation of the darkened state of her nipples.

He was right. This kiss was nothing like the last one.

This kiss was like the ones she remembered. Sort of.

Bess whimpered a little as his lips opened and Wade's tongue stroked against hers. There was something more raw about the raggedness of his breathing, the urgency in his hands as they stroked her face. Her hair.

Maybe she wasn't the only one who came to this cabin a little different.

This wasn't the same man she remembered. Similar, but still different.

And different wasn't always a bad thing.

She wasn't quite ready when Wade pulled away. "Where are you going?"

"Relax, Sweetheart. I'm not leaving you. Not again." He eased off her body and off the bed. "I'm going to try to make you a little more comfortable."

Bess watched as he went to the switch beside the door and flipped it, blanketing the room in darkness.

"Wade?"

"God I love it when you say my name." His voice was already closer. A second later a dim light barely illuminated him. "I hated hearing you say another man's name that night, you know that?"

Whitt. It was the name he gave her when they first met. "I knew it wasn't your name."

Wade stood from where he'd switched on the small night light plugged into the wall. "Did you?"

Bess nodded. "I knew you were leaving. I knew you gave me a fake name. I knew it all."

It was why she could never really be mad at him. Wade never once made her think that night would be more than it was.

And she hadn't wanted it to be. Hell, she'd even told him directly it would never be more.

"I don't want you to feel bad for what happened. I knew going into it I would never see you again." And she'd tried to be okay with it.

But then Parker made that impossible.

Not that it wouldn't have happened anyway.

Even if Parker hadn't come along, she would have tried to find him eventually, for reasons she still didn't fully understand.

Wade came back toward the bed, each step raising the pace of her heart. "I will feel bad for what happened. You can't stop that."

"You shouldn't."

"I shouldn't feel bad that I left you and our son?" Wade's knee rested on the mattress, followed by the other. "I should have been there to protect you." He dropped to his hands and prowled closer. "I should have been there to take care of you."

Bess swallowed as he moved back over her. "I thought you said you weren't good for me."

Wade's body settled against hers. "I think I was wrong."

"Because of Parker?"

His head barely moved from side to side. "No, Sweetheart. Because of you."

Her eyes fell closed as he leaned in again.

She waited for the feel of his lips.

It didn't come.

"Why aren't you kissing me, Wade?"

"You never told me I could."

"You were kissing me just a second ago."

He chuckled low. "I was, wasn't I?"

Bess waited a second longer before opening her eyes. "Please kiss me."

"Just kissing?" His lips barely brushed hers. "Or can I see this supposedly less-than-perfect body you've been telling me about?"

She'd been brave that night with him. Let him keep the lights on and everything. It felt empowering in the moment, but now it meant he had expectations.

One's she could no longer fulfill.

"Relax." Wade's lips moved over her face, along the line of her jaw. "We've got plenty of time." His mouth paused against her ear. "But make no mistake, I intend to see and worship every fucking inch of this body soon, Sweetheart."

Bess shivered as his lips coasted down her neck. "There's a little more territory to cover than last time."

"Perfect." His hands were moving over her body, running along the fuller line of her hips, the wider curve of her thighs. Pregnancy had filled out areas that no amount of stress dieting could reduce back to their starting size. "I love this spot right here." His thumb skimmed under the hem of her shirt, stroking the lined skin of her belly. "You're skin is so damn soft."

"I moisturize." What in the hell was she saying? Why was this so much more difficult than last time?

"Bess." Wade's tone was a little sharp as he leaned up to look her in the eye. "I spent the last two years kicking myself for letting you get away. If you think I am anything less than fucking thrilled to have to under me again, then you are very wrong." His lips dropped to meet hers in a short, but heated kiss. "I tried to be with other women, you know that?"

She couldn't stop the frown his revelation twisted onto her lips.

Wade laughed softly. "I like that look on your face, Sweetheart, but it's unwarranted." He kissed her again, this time a little longer. "I couldn't get it up. Not one damn time."

Bess looked between their bodies again to the spot where his definitely erect dick pressed against her belly, hard and thick through the fabric of his jeans. "But—"

"I couldn't even make myself do it if I wanted to, and I hate to admit it, but there were times where I really fucking wanted to." He kissed what was left of the spot between her brows. The gap was nearly gone by the depth of the frown she couldn't seem to stop.

"But I only fucking wanted you." His lips moved over one brow to her temple. "Can you imagine what that was like? Wanting something you knew you should never fucking have again?"

"Maybe that's why you wanted me." The possibility settled in her belly, cold and heavy. "Maybe it was because you couldn't have me."

And now that he could—

"That's not it. You know damn well it's not." The sharpness was back in his tone. "It doesn't make sense. I know that." Wade's eyes were on hers, impossibly black in the dimly-lit room. "But that doesn't mean it's not real."

Bess swallowed hard around the ball of fear clogging her throat. She'd built this man up in her mind for two years. Made him into anything she wanted him to be.

What if he was nothing like she imagined? What if the real Wade fell short?

Worse yet, what if she did?

"What if it's not what we think it is?"

Wade's hands came to the sides of her face, smoothing back the strands of her hair as they stroked across her skin. "Then we'll work through it." His lips lifted into a barely-there smile that stole her breath with its honesty. "But I meant what I said earlier, Bess." His expression turned serious. "You and Parker are mine."

"What if he's not?" It was the single most terrifying thought she owned. One that kept her awake at night and sick to her stomach all day.

What if the way Parker looked was due to some sort of recessive gene? What if Chris *was* his father?

The seriousness in Wade's eyes intensified, shifting into the version of him she saw earlier today when the two men appeared. "I don't give a shit who gave you Parker. I will protect him, Bess. No one will fucking hurt him again."

Bess stared up at him in disbelief.

The night they'd met she was looking for a distraction. Something to show her that there were better men out there than the one she was trying to leave behind.

Than Chris.

By some twist of fate she found Wade, and he showed her a man could be more. Attentive. Sweet. Protective. Complimentary. Even that first night, he gave her things she'd never had before.

But this was above and beyond.

"Why?"

"I fucked up once with you, Bess. I'm not doing it again." His smile was back, only this time it held a completely different sort of emotion. "And you're locked in a cabin with me for the foreseeable future, so I have plenty of time to show you how good it could be if you decided to let me take care of you."

"To let you?"

"You're in charge, Bess. Always." His already devilish smile took on a wicked slant. "I'm at your mercy."

"I thought you were the one in control?" There was something about the idea that held a certain amount of appeal, she wasn't going to pretend differently.

"Definitely." Wade's lips brushed hers as one hand skimmed down her body. "As long as I'm good at what I do you won't even think of telling me to stop." His fingers worked the button on her pants. "And I plan on being very good." The fastener came loose and the sound of the zipper teeth separating almost echoed in the room.

"Who's made you come since I did, Bess?" His hand eased into the opening he made.

"No one." She could barely get the words out as his fingers teased the top of her pubic bone through the cotton of her panties.

"I'm sure that's not true." His voice was low in her ear as his hand pushed into her pants a little more. "I'm positive at the very least you've touched yourself. Isn't that right?" He stroked along the seam of her pussy, the barrier of her panties keeping the touch from being more than a tickling tease.

"Yes." She whimpered as his hand pulled free.

"I promised to take care of you, Sweetheart. I meant it. Just trust me." His hand was back, sliding under the elastic band of the blue flowered granny-panties she'd taken to wearing since Parker's birth. "Who did you think of when you played with your pussy?" His touch immediately went right where she wanted it, finding her clit and stroking a few times before stopping.

Bess gasped in frustration. "Don't stop."

Wade leaned in, lips brushing her ear. "Then tell me who you thought of when you touched yourself."

"You." She'd have confessed all her dirty little fantasies if it meant he would finish what he started.

"Who else?" He continued to withhold his touch.

And it sort of pissed her off. Two fucking years of supposedly thinking of her and he was going to tease her like this? Fine. "Henry Cavill."

Wade's eyes narrowed on hers. "The fuck is Henry Cavill?"

She smirked up at him, feeling a little proud of her ability to irritate him as well as he was irritating her. "He's Superman."

Wade's head tipped to one side in obvious confusion. "Who?"

"Do you live in a hole? He's the actor who plays Superman and he's beautiful."

Wade's nostrils barely flared. "Beautiful, huh?"

She nodded. "Very."

Wade's fingers started to move again, this time with purpose.

"I bet he can't make you scream his fucking name."

CHAPTER 7

IF THERE WAS ever anything in the world that could make him lose his cool it was this woman.

Bess pushed him in ways no one ever had.

The idea of her even thinking of another man while she came made him want to drop bodies.

That wasn't normal. Not even for him.

"I only want to hear *my* name come out of your mouth when you come, understand me?"

Wade wanted to strip her naked, lick and suck every inch of her until he was the only man she knew.

But right now Bess doubted his desire for her. Doubted he would find her as perfect today as he did two years ago.

So he would be as patient as he had the ability to be. "Who am I, Bess?"

"Wade."

The way she said it was enough to make him hate the insecurity he created. The wall it put between them. A wall that hadn't been there two years ago.

He'd left her once. For nothing more than his own convoluted belief that he wouldn't be able to keep her safe.

And he was right. He hadn't.

"Say it again." He needed to burn away the memory of another man's name on her lips. He'd carried it with him since that night.

It was time for it to die. All of it.

The lies he told. The lies she gave him back.

"Wade." It barely made it out before she gasped as his finger slid inside her body. "Please don't stop."

He had no intention to stop anything else that would happen between them. Maybe move slow. Maybe be careful. But he would never stop when it came to Bess.

Not again.

"You were meant to be mine, Bess. I knew it that first fucking night and I should have listened. I would have been there." He couldn't keep his mouth shut. Couldn't stop the confessions falling from his lips. "I would have kept you from him. I swear I would have."

"Shut up." Her back barely arched as he found her clit with his thumb, pulling a soft sound from her throat.

He pressed his lips together in an attempt to stop the words from flowing.

It didn't help. He couldn't make himself quit talking to her. "You feel so good." Wade curled his

90

fingers, finding the spot he knew would give him what he wanted, and stroked it relentlessly.

"Wade!" His name jumped free as her thighs jerked.

"That's it, Sweetheart. I want my name on your lips when you come for me. Give it to me." He leaned up to look at her, taking in the tousled mass of her blonde hair. The fullness of her kiss-swollen mouth. The glazed look in Bessie's hooded gaze as her eyes found his.

And there it was.

The connection neither could deny.

He didn't look away as her body started to tremble.

Her eyes stayed on his as her pussy started to clench around his fingers, tight with impending release.

She came, eyes locked onto his, her sweet voice filling the room with his name.

Only when her lids fell closed did he look away, running his lips over any bit of skin bared to him. "You are still just as perfect, Bess." Wade eased free of her body, sliding his hand from her pants. "So damn beautiful."

He kissed over her cheeks, her neck, her temple, trying to get enough of her to tide him over until morning. "I should let you go to sleep." He glanced at the clock on the nightstand. "Jesus, it's after two."

He'd been up almost twenty-four hours which was nothing unusual, but he was nowhere near as tired as he should be. It was more than he could say for the woman beside him.

Bess yawned, one hand coming up to cover her mouth. "I'm so tired all of a sudden." She rolled to her side and curled around him.

"It's late." He should go upstairs, leave her to sleep. Instead Wade shifted closer, wrapping an arm around her and pulling Bess against him.

"I don't usually sleep well, though. I'm always up past two." She yawned again. "Without a nap."

"Then you should go to sleep while you can." He pressed a kiss to her hair, working up the motivation to leave her bed and her room. "I'll go." He started to ease away.

"What?" Bess shot up into a sit. "You're leaving?"

Wade froze.

It didn't occur to him she might feel like history was repeating itself. "Not leaving, Sweetheart. Just thought you'd want to get some sleep."

"What are you going to do?"

"I was going upstairs to take a shower and then I'm going to get some sleep too."

She let out a breath. "You're coming back then."

"Is that what you want? Me in here with you?" Wade tried to keep his tone indifferent. There was nothing he wanted more than to sleep beside her. Be close in case she and Parker needed him, but the ball was going to have to be in her court for a long time.

Bess nodded. "I think I'll sleep better knowing you're close."

It wasn't as definite of a desire as he carried, but it was close enough. Wade brushed a kiss over

92

her lips. "I'll take a quick shower and then I'll be right back."

Bess smiled softly. "Okay."

Wade backed out of the room, leaving the door cracked as he left. As soon as he was out of her sight, he turned and raced up the stairs. Ten minutes later he was showered and in a pair of jersey joggers and a t-shirt, trying to shake the remaining water from his hair as he hurried back down the stairs.

The glow of the fridge stopped him halfway down. Bessie's small form was illuminated against the open door. "Hungry?"

She shook her head. "Thirsty." A second later she had a water bottle in hand as she knocked the door shut with one hip. She stood still for a minute in the dark. "Wade?"

"What's wrong, Sweetheart?" The tightness of her voice had him moving again.

"This house is really freaking dark."

"I'm coming. Just stand still." He reached her side just as she started laughing. "Why does it suddenly seem so dark in here?"

"Your head was just in the fridge." He rested one hand on the small of her back. "Your eyes will adjust in just a minute." He added a little pressure to his touch. "You'll probably be okay in a few days when you're used to the layout."

"This is a really nice cabin." Bess leaned into his side a little, letting him guide her along. "Is it the only one?"

"Alaskan Security has ten in Brisbane, and a few more scattered around the state." Wade maneuvered Bess around the large leather sectional in the great room, and past the set of oversized armchairs toward the door to the master.

"Why Alaska? Why not someplace like California?" Bess didn't move away as they stepped into the soft light of the bedroom night light.

"Because it's huge and intimidating. Most people don't like to come here, especially in the winter." Wade silently closed the door and locked the deadbolt. "Means the chances of our clients being bothered is slim to none."

Bessie's eyes went to the motion. "So I'm in the spot someone is least likely to find me." Her eyes slowly lifted to his. "And they found me the first day."

It was a fact he was working hard not to think about. "No one will touch you, Bess."

"How did he find me?" The panic in her eyes cut into the deepest part of him.

"We don't know for sure those men were looking for you." Wade stepped close. "It could have been a fluke." He decided to leave out the shot they took at him. Luckily he sent her to the safe room, so there was no way Bess could have heard the gunfire.

She nodded. "I can't really imagine Chris would ever come someplace like this anyway."

"That's probably true." He went with her assessment, hoping Bess could talk herself out of the fear still shimmering in her gaze. "It's not very nice up here."

She lifted one shoulder. "I don't know." She twisted the cap off her water. "It's really pretty."

"It's cold as hell though." Wade rested his hands on the soft flannel covering her hips. "I'm glad you came prepared."

Bess glanced down at her pajamas. "I get cold at night."

"Then tonight's your lucky night." He scooped her up and carried her to the bed, ignoring the pang of guilt her tiny frame twisted inside him. "Because I'm a cuddler."

She laughed as he yanked back the covers and settled her between the sheets. "I don't remember that."

Wade hesitated as the truth tried to come out. He wanted her to see him differently, and reminding her of his bad behavior that night wouldn't help his cause.

But neither would lying about it.

"I left as soon as you were asleep." He took her bottle of water and set it on the nightstand. "I knew if I laid with you I wouldn't leave."

There were so many little things that could have changed the way that night went. If he'd done any one of them he would have been there. Seen her belly grow. Seen his son born. Watched his first steps.

Bess touched his face. Her hands were warm and soft. "Then I guess you'll be disappointed to find out that I am not a cuddler."

Christ but she was more perfect than he deserved.

Wade eased into the bed beside her. "I think I can convert you."

****

THE SOUND OF Parker rolling in his crib woke him in an instant.

Wade didn't move. Just listened to the soft sound of Parker's little body as he worked himself awake. The room was still dark, and it would be hours before the glow of sunrise began to shift the shadows. Bess was curled tight against him, putting off enough heat to melt all the snow in Alaska.

He smiled into her hair. Didn't like to cuddle his ass.

Wade waited until Parker's little head popped up, taking in as much of the moment as he could before slipping free of the arm Bess had thrown over his chest, and off the bed. Parker watched him with focused eyes as he moved toward the crib. When he reached the side, Wade bent down and held out his hands. "You wanna get up?"

Parker nodded and reached for him, letting his head fall on Wade's shoulder as he walked out of the room and into the kitchen. "You hungry, Buddy?" He opened the fridge and pulled out a carton of eggs. "Scrambled or fried?"

"Scrambled." Brock padded across the tile floor, his boxer briefs hanging low on his waist. He stopped when he saw Wade glaring at him. "What?"

"Put some fucking clothes on."

Brock pointed to Parker. "Your kid's first word is going to be fuck."

"He says momma." Wade shifted Parker to his hip as he opened the eggs and grabbed a bowl from the cabinet.

"Fine." Brock grabbed the coffee pot off the maker and filled it with water. "His second word then."

Wade cracked ten eggs into the bowl one-handed, managing to only end up having to fish out one small chunk of shell. "You checked the weather?"

"Not since before bed. Supposed to hit around lunchtime last I checked." Brock loaded up the coffee grounds and pushed the brew button before leaning back against the counter. "You hear anything from Dutch?"

Wade glanced around the room. "Shit." He must have left his phone in the office last night. "I hope not." He retrieved his cell, checking it on his way back to the kitchen. There were ten messages from Dutch.

"Looks like they found video of the sled on a trailer headed out of town." Wade skimmed the rest of the messages. "Said it looked like two were in the cab of the truck hauling it, so it could be our guys." He held the phone out to Brock.

"Leaving already?" Brock took the phone and thumbed through the text string. "Maybe someone had old information."

They didn't usually run into overlap. When they were done with a client it was because the threat was over, but that didn't mean their client base didn't usually find themselves in the middle of a new mess. "Who was here last?"

Brock's fingers moved over the screen of Wade's phone. "I'll find out."

A few minutes later Dutch texted back just as Wade was finishing up the eggs. Brock scanned the screen. "Armondo."

"Well shit." There went the theory that it was someone after the previous client who stayed here. "Armondo's been dead what, two months now?"

Brock poured a cup of coffee and slid it across the counter to where Wade was setting Parker up in his high chair. "He probably shouldn't have fired us."

"He's not the first." It happened more often than it should. A client would decide that because no one had tried to off them while Rogue was watching, that they weren't in danger anymore. Each time Dutch would find proof they were and try to explain, but occasionally a client would think they knew better.

It's probably what landed them needing Team Rogue in the first place.

"So unless they're dumb as hell, they aren't here looking for Armondo." Wade sipped at the screaming hot coffee, making sure to put it well out of Parker's reach before turning his attention to helping the little boy with his eggs.

"What are you gonna do, man?"

Wade shook his head. "Probably call Dutch later. See what else he can find."

"I'm not talking about that." Brock came to sit in the stool on the other side of Parker's chair. "I'm talking about little man here."

Wade watched as Parker fisted in a handful of eggs, his dark eyes squinting as he grinned around the food. "I'm going to take care of them."

"So he is yours?"

Wade grabbed the toast he made to go with the eggs and started tearing it into bite-sized pieces. "I'm not sure I care."

Brock's head bobbed back. "Wow."

Wade dropped a few pieces of the buttered toast onto the tray. "I think I might leave the team."

"You want to leave?" Brock frowned at him across Parker's head. "I knew you weren't happy, but I didn't realize it was that bad."

"What if Bessie's situation was reversed?"

Brock's brows came together in confusion. "You mean if she was trying to get at him?"

"No. I mean what if maybe her dad was trying to kill him for hurting her and Parker, and Chris was the one who hired us." He met Brock's eyes. "What then? We just protect a batterer?"

Brock held his gaze. "We have before."

Wade shifted in his seat as Parker watched him with eyes that seemed to see so much more than they should be able to. "I don't think I can do that anymore."

It was something he was struggling with even before Bess. At least back then he could push it away. Shove the reality of what he did for a living out of his mind.

But it got harder. Knowing the men he protected didn't always deserve it. Frequently didn't appreciate it.

Now that he'd seen the other side it would be impossible.

Brock nodded. "I know what you mean." His eyes dipped to Parker for a second before coming back to Wade's. "You saying you wouldn't be able to kill anyone again?"

Wade reached out to smooth down Parker's dark hair. "Definitely not saying that."

He would happily put another man in the ground. And any after that who might try to take away what he just found.

What he just realized he wanted.

"You didn't wake me up."

Both men stood in unison as Bess came into the kitchen. She lifted a brow at Brock's bare chest before turning to Wade and Parker. "You could have woken me up."

"You need to get more sleep." He glanced down as Parker caught the pocket of his pants and pulled. "We're fine. He's eating breakfast."

"I see that." Bess settled into the seat Wade vacated. "Has he had a fresh diaper?"

"He has not." Wade pressed his lips into a line. "I should have probably done that first."

"Have you ever changed a diaper?" Bess dusted toast crumbs off Parker's nose.

"It can't be that difficult." Wade held out his hands for Parker. "Come on, Buddy. Let's go get you situated."

Parker immediately reached for him. Wade tucked the little boy into one arm and nodded to the pan of eggs. "Brock will get you all set up with something to eat."

Brock rounded the island, a shit-eating grin on his face. "I'd be happy to service our guest."

"Don't make me kill a man in front of a baby." Wade pointed at his friend. "And put a damn shirt on. She doesn't want to look at your nipples while she eats."

Brock rubbed one palm over a nipple. "What's wrong with my nipples?"

"Your nipples are just fine." Bess narrowed her eyes at Wade. "Ignore him."

"He's just jealous because his are hairy as shit." Brock dropped two pieces of bread in the toaster as Bess tilted her head to one side.

"I thought you were making me biscuits and gravy for breakfast."

Wade started laughing as he made his way toward the bedroom where all Parker's stuff was. "Better make her some gravy." He stopped and turned to face his friend. "And put a freaking shirt on."

CHAPTER 8

BESS PEEKED AROUND the door frame into the bedroom where Wade was attempting to change Parker's diaper.

"Come on, Buddy. Help me out here." Wade struggled to wrangle Parker's flailing arms and kicking legs. "We gotta show her I'm more than a pretty face." He finally managed to get the breakfast-covered sleeper off her son's wiggly body, dropping it to the floor at his feet as he continued to grapple with Parker.

Wade started to open the diaper.

"Wait."

He and Parker both jumped a little, each craning to look her way.

She stepped in beside Wade at the edge of the tall bed that worked perfectly as a make-shift changing table. "The second the cold air hits his stuff he will pee." She shook open a fresh diaper, using it as a guard as she slipped the other one off.

"You're kidding." Wade leaned down to look at Parker. "You do that to your momma?"

"Ma-ma-ma-ma-ma-ma." Parker grabbed at the new diaper as Bess tried to strap on the sticky strips.

"I'd rather that than the other." She reached for an outfit from the pile of Parker's clothes stacked on the dresser then pulled a long-sleeved shirt over his head.

"The other?" Wade took the socks she chose and worked them onto Parker's feet.

"Poop. He's pooped on me more times than I can count." Bess waited while Wade fought the second sock into place.

His lips pressed into a thin line as he watched her tug Parker's jeans over his legs and snap them.

Bess hefted Parker off the bed, pressing a kiss to his head. "There. Better?" When she glanced up, Wade was watching her.

"You shouldn't have been doing it alone."

She heaved out a sigh. "I made the same choices you did."

Wade shook his head. "I could have found you and I didn't. There was no way for you to find me."

Bess faced him completely. "If you knew about Parker, would it have changed anything?"

"Of course it would have." His answer was immediate.

Her eyes dropped his. "That's good then."

He would have come for Parker.

Just not her.

The realization stung, especially since she'd admitted her reasons for wanting to find him weren't only because of Parker.

He'd said he didn't plan to ever try to find her, and apparently he meant it.

Bess backed toward the door, needing a little space. "The gravy's probably done." She turned and rushed from the room before Wade could see what she hoped to hide.

"Bess." His tone was soft and filled with regret.

She kept going.

Passing through the kitchen, she handed Parker off to Brock. "Can you take him for a minute?" Without giving him an option she continued on, needing to find a spot where she could be alone.

Could process everything piling up around her.

Bess moved through the house, not really knowing where she was going, just trying to get away from all of it.

The stress. The fear. The burdens she'd been carrying for so damn long.

"Where's Bess?" Wade's voice was far behind her, muffled by the turns she'd taken to end up where she was.

Which appeared to be a mudroom of sorts. White coats and coveralls hung from hooks lined down the wall. Matching white boots sat on the tile under the outerwear.

That was a lot of white, which didn't seem practical.

"Bess?" Wade's voice was closer now.

She needed to think. Needed to cry probably. And neither of those were things she could or would do with him there.

Bess grabbed one of the coats and pulled it on over her flannel pajamas as she shoved her feet into a pair of boots. Even the smallest-looking of the bunch was huge on her, but she didn't have time to find appropriate footwear.

She just needed a few minutes to herself. Then it would all be fine again.

The door beeped three times as she yanked it open.

"Shit." She should have known there would be an alarm system. Too late to worry about it now.

The first step outside stole her breath.

"Holy fuck, it's cold." Tucking her nose and mouth into the high collar of the coat, Bess trudged through the fresh layer of snow falling across the deck.

Was there nowhere warm to hide her? Maybe a beach somewhere? At least then she would be sandy and sad.

Tears pricked her already burning eyes. She knew damn well Wade's guilt all rested on her son's little head.

Parker was the reason he wished he'd looked for her. It had nothing to do with her. Not really. Because at the end of the day she wasn't worth whatever sacrifice finding her would bring him.

Parker was. And she should be grateful Wade felt that way.

Which was why she was stomping through snow that reached her knees.

She was a terrible mother. Jealous of her own child. Butt hurt that he could accomplish what she couldn't.

The tears fell fast, chilling her already half-frozen face. The guilt and embarrassment of her horrible feelings made her stomach burn.

Bess rounded the corner of the cabin, hoping to find some sort of place she could hunker down and have a good cry. It always made her feel better. Getting it all out. Then she could put on her big-girl panties and march on.

Unfortunately, the only thing on the side of the cabin was a bank of huge fir trees, branches hanging low with the weight of the falling snow. "Damn it."

She continued her heavy-footed trek toward them. It was the best she was going to get. Maybe if she squeezed into them and sat against the cabin it wouldn't be too bad. At least she could be alone.

An odd sound came from right beside her, the strange whooshing muffled by the heavy hood of her coat. Bess had to turn her whole body to look in the direction it came from.

There was nothing there.

She started to move again, but stumbled, almost dropping to the snow-covered ground. As she caught herself with both hands, the strange sound came again, this time over her head. "What in the—"

An instant later she was face first in the snow, knocked down by a force strong enough to punch the air from her lungs. The same sound as before came again, this time in quick succession as her whole body was rolled toward the trees she'd been eyeing. The world spun until branches scraped her cheeks and pine needles poked through her red plaid pajama pants, stabbing into her skin.

A heavy hand came over her mouth, pressing tight.

Bess took a breath, ready to put her whole self behind the scream she was building.

"Shhh." An arm snaked around her waist, pulling her body back against a solid wall. "You've gotta be quiet, Sweetheart."

Wade.

Bess watched from under the trees as the sound continued and puffs of snow kicked up from the ground.

Oh God.

It was bullets. Someone was shooting.

At her.

Wade's hand eased from her mouth, moving to wrap across her chest, pulling her deeper into the trees as the gunfire seemed to get louder.

"They're getting closer." She pressed back into Wade, trying to get as far away from the edge of the trees as possible.

"That's not them." He pulled her in tighter, wrapping one leg over hers, managing to almost completely cover her body with his. "It's Brock." Wade reached behind his back. When his arm came back over her there was a pistol in his hand. "He will handle it. We just have to wait."

"What about Parker?" Panic gripped her gut and squeezed, shoving the contents of her stomach burning their way up her throat.

"Parker is safe." He leaned in close, the side of his face resting against the side of hers with the heavy canvas of her hood between them. "You didn't give me the chance to explain."

Was he really doing this now? When someone was trying to shoot her? "I don't want to talk about it."

"You have something else to do?" Wade nuzzled against the crook of her neck. "If you'd stayed long enough to listen to what I had to say, you would have heard that knowing about Parker would have given me the excuse I was looking for." His head barely lifted from hers as the sounds disappeared. "The weight of one guilt would have trumped the weight of the other."

"It's fine." She sniffled as her nose started to run. The coat was well-insulated, but no match for the cold ground, and her teeth were starting to chatter as her body temperature dropped.

"What's happening right now? This is my life, Bess. This is what I would have been dragging you into." Wade held her so tight she could barely breathe. "It would have been selfish as fuck of me to do that to you."

"But I'm here anyway." She sniffed again, only this time it had nothing to do with the cold. "You left for nothing."

She'd been alone. Pregnant and on her own. Her family was there of course, but it wasn't the same.

A pair of naked legs sticking out of a pair of boots that matched the ones she had on walked along the tree line. Brock's face peered at them from under the bottom row of branches. He reached one hand toward her. "Come on. I'm fucking freezing."

Bess took his hand and let Brock help her shimmy across the pile of needles matting into her pants. As soon as she was clear, he hefted her to her feet.

"You're naked." She blinked at his goosebump-covered chest. "Why are you naked?"

Brock snapped the waistband of his underwear as his brown eyes scanned the yard. "Not naked." He reached for Wade, jerking him to his feet before stepping in front of her. "Come on."

Wade was at her back, hands on her waist as he pressed her close to Brock, who had a rifle of some sort propped and ready. They quickly made their way up the side of the cabin and across the deck. Brock punched a series of numbers into the keypad before opening the door, wrapping one arm around her and taking her inside with him.

Then the door shut behind her.

With Wade still outside.

"Wait. Wade's not inside." She grabbed at the handle, trying to get the door back open.

"He's fine, Bess." Brock's arm at her waist held tight, pulling her deeper into the cabin and away from the door. "The rest of the team will be here any second."

"But there's someone shooting out there." The words were barely out of her mouth when the glass of the door window split, sending tiny slivers onto the tile floor.

Bess only got a glimpse of the hole in the center of the spider web of cracks before Brock spun her away, hauling her through the house and into the bedroom where he shoved her into the safe room where Parker was sitting in his portable crib. "Lock the door, Bess. You know the rules on coming out."

Then he was gone, slamming the door behind him.

She flipped the deadbolt on the safe room for the second time in two days, and pulled Parker from the crib, tucking him against her chest as she sank to the floor, burying her face in his little neck as she tried to breathe.

Was Chris really this determined to punish her for leaving him? Willing to kill her to prove a point?

It sure as hell seemed that way.

How could she not have seen it? Years she was with him, never once suspecting the kind of monster he hid beneath sleek suits and smooth words.

It was always there though if she'd known what to look for.

The way he was disconnected from anything that didn't matter to him. The cold edge he had when something didn't go his way.

His ability to never be at fault.

She rocked from side to side, trying to calm herself in the complete silence of the small room.

The whole world could be falling apart on the other side of the steel door and she would never know.

Wade could be hurt.

Shot. Bleeding in the snow.

Because of her.

Did he even have a coat on?

Brock certainly didn't.

"Bess? It's Abe." The voice over the speaker had her on her feet in an instant. Her hand was on the deadbolt when he stopped her. "Don't open the door yet."

She punched the button. "Why not?"

"Just don't."

She pulled Parker closer. "Is there someone in the house?"

"Everything is okay, just don't open the door yet."

She stared at the speaker. Abe said everything was okay, but the tone of his voice sure sounded like there was something wrong. Something that he didn't want her to see.

"Oh no." She flipped the deadbolt and was out of the room, rushing through the house with Abe on her heels.

"Bess. Stop."

"Where is he?" She ran straight for the group of men in white standing clustered around one of the chairs at the kitchen island and shoved her way through. "Move." When her eyes landed on him, she sucked in a breath.

Wade was sitting perfectly still in the high-top chair, eyes closed, while a tall man with a tight fade shoved a needle through a slice across the outside of his arm. Abe caught her as she started to tip back. "He's fine, Bess."

"That's not fine." Her voice wavered.

And it pissed her off.

All of this pissed her off.

"He's not fucking fine." It wasn't quite a yell.

Maybe it was.

Whatever.

She was so freaking over all of this.

The man sewing Wade's arm glanced her way, the clear blue of his eyes a striking contrast to the dark brown of his skin. He shot her a grin. "She's cute, Wade."

"Shut up and stitch, Tyson." Wade's lids lifted and his dark eyes immediately found her and Parker. He held his free hand out. "Come here."

She didn't hesitate, immediately going to his side, eyeing the rest of him as she went.

There weren't any more obvious wounds, so that was good.

He reached for her face, cradling it as the pad of his thumb stroked the corner of her mouth. "I'm fine." He glanced at where Tyson was tying off the thread. "It just grazed me."

"You were shot?" Bess looked to Tyson. "He was shot?"

Tyson was busy bandaging the injury. "Doesn't count as shot unless the bullet actually goes in."

"What?" She looked around the faces of the men filling the kitchen. "Shot is shot."

Nate shook his head. "Team rules. You only get to claim being shot if the bullet goes in."

Bess motioned to the spot Tyson was taping up. "What in the hell do you call that then?"

"We call this a scratch." Tyson gave her a wink.

"See?" Wade pulled her close. "It's just a scratch."

She was surrounded by crazy men who ran around shooting people in their underwear in sub-zero weather and called gunshots scratches.

Brock shouldered his way toward her. He was finally dressed. She stared at his all-white cargo pants and long-sleeved fitted white shirt. "You think you're going to have to go outside again."

It wasn't a question. Twice already there had been someone outside the cabin no one was supposed to be able to find her in. "That's why all the coats are white."

"Smart *and* cute." Tyson wiggled his brows at her. "A double threat."

"I will kick your ass one armed." Wade stood from the chair, wrapping his uninjured arm tight around her and Parker.

Tyson held his hands up. "I'm not trying to take your lady, Wade." He leaned in toward Bess. "But if you have any friends I'd be more than happy to occupy a little of their time."

"I'm not from here." She decided to go with that explanation rather than admit that she only had one friend who was happily married to a wonderful man.

And very far away.

Tyson sighed dramatically. "Damn."

"Striking out again." Brock slapped Tyson on the shoulder. "Maybe you can go with me to

114

Florida next time. The odds are better there. Ratio of women to men is in our favor." Brock's eyes narrowed for just a second as the whole room went quiet. His eyes slid her way, barely stalling before stopping on Wade. "Got it."

"Who is he talking to?" Bess looked to Wade.

"Probably Dutch." He watched Brock closely, his whole body tight. "He's our tech guy. Watches all our cameras and everyone else's."

Brock barely nodded Wade's way and the rigidness of his frame eased. "Come on, Sweetheart." Wade pulled her toward the bedroom. "Call me if you need me." He led her into the room, following close behind. When the door was closed she spun to face him.

"You were shot."

"Don't let them hear you say that." Wade walked to the bathroom and she followed behind him, waiting as he pulled open one of the mirrored medicine cabinets and pulled out a bottle of ibuprofen, popping a few into his mouth before leaning down to drink straight from the faucet.

"Why would Chris shoot you?"

Wade straightened, his lips pressing into a thin line as he stared at her in silence.

Finally he wiped one hand down his face, blowing out a long breath.

"Bess Sweetheart, I'm not sure this is Chris we're dealing with."

CHAPTER 9

BESS WENT PALE.

"What are you talking about? It has to be Chris. Who else would it be?"

No one else wanted to tell her, and if it had been anyone else Wade would have agreed with them.

But this was Bess.

"Chris is an ass. I'm not arguing that." Wade moved in close, needing to feel her against him. His heart had nearly stopped when he shut off the house alarm only to realize it wasn't the only one going off. Knowing Bess wasn't alone outside was the first time he'd ever really felt panic. "But would he really be willing to go this far?"

She rubbed her lips together, clearly thinking her way through the situation.

He leaned into her, holding Bess and Parker with his good arm as he rested his forehead against the top of her head. "You scared the shit out of me, Sweetheart."

"I didn't know there was anyone out there." The tiny bit of defiance in her tone made him smile in spite of the lingering fear gnawing at him. "I wouldn't have gone outside if I knew." Her head tipped back, hazel eyes squinting a little as she looked up at him. "Why didn't you know someone was out there?"

"The perimeter alarm started going off at the same time you set off the house alarm." He pressed into her, pushing Bess back into the bedroom. All he wanted was to hold her and Parker for a minute. "I would have had you earlier, but I had to make sure Parker was safe."

He'd yelled back at Brock and taken off at a full run at the sound of the first silenced shot, barely able to breathe as he watched the shots tag the snow around her.

Bess backed along with him toward the bed. "Thank you for that."

He gave her a small nod. "I knew it's what you would want me to do." Wade rested one of his hands on Parker's back. "He's a trooper."

Her smile flattened into a thin line. "He's had to be."

"It's almost over, Bess." Wade bumped into her, knocking her butt to the bed. "Dutch will figure out what's going on and the rest of us will handle it."

One of her pale brows lifted. "The rest of you?"

Wade held her around the waist with his good arm and tried to maneuver her body toward the center of the bed. Even that small movement made him wince.

She scooted out of his grip. "I can't believe you got yourself shot." The flat line of her mouth tipped into a frown. One he'd seen a lot of in the last twenty-four hours.

"It'll only be sore for a day. Then I'll be good as new." Wade eased down beside her.

"You say that like you have experience." Bessie's eyes moved over his body.

"I don't make a habit of getting shot, Sweetheart. Not many people I would take a bullet for." Wade reached for her with his good arm. "Come here."

She hesitated, hazel gaze moving to the injured limb between them. "Won't it hurt your arm?"

"It's worth it." He grabbed her and tugged her into his chest. Parker immediately popped back up and started worming his way toward the edge of the mattress.

"It's not his nap time." Bess snagged Parker's arm just as he attempted to slide over one side. "You want some toys?"

Parker's head bobbed around as he crawled toward the small pile of toys on the dresser.

"He's going to need more to play with." Wade pushed up. He was crashing from the adrenaline rush and all he wanted to do was lie with Bess. Hold her close.

But it didn't look like it was in the cards.

"You good in here for a few minutes? I want to go see what they found." It was time to figure out a way to get Bess and Parker somewhere else.

Someplace safe.

Bess glanced down at her trashed pajama bottoms. "I should probably change." She helped Parker slide off the bed, supporting him until he had his feet under him.

Wade watched as Parker toddled toward him, his pajama-covered feet shuffling across the carpet as he went. The little boy stopped at his feet and raised both arms over his head, opening and closing his fingers. "Up."

"You don't have to—"

Wade dropped to a squat and scooped Parker up with his uninjured arm. "You wanna hang out with the boys, Buddy?" He looked to Bess, making sure it was okay.

She gave him a little nod. "Thank you."

"Nothing you have to thank me for." Wade leaned back a little, looking Parker in the eye. "Let's let your momma have a minute to herself, okay?"

"Ma-ma-ma-ma." Parker bounced a little in his hold.

"That's right." Wade gave Bess a wink. "We gotta take care of your momma."

He went to the office where most of the team was gathered with the exception of Abe and Jamison. Wade eased into one of the empty chairs around the long table situated at one end of the room. "Abe and Jamison fixing the door?"

Brock had his feet propped up on the table, looking as comfortable as Wade would if this situation involved just another client. "They've almost got the new one in."

Dutch was setting up at the large desk taking up the other end of the room, unpacking multiple laptops from a large black bag. "I think our girl has more enemies than she's letting on, Wade."

Dutch wasn't one to mince words. Probably because he didn't have time. His job description kept growing along with Alaskan Security.

"What did you find?"

Dutch dropped into the large leather desk chair and started punching the keys of one of the boards in front of him. "This was a different set of guys today." He spun one of the monitors to face Wade as one of the security videos from the cabin's system started to play. "There were five this time. I can't believe they didn't hit her."

Wade watched as the set of five men carefully picked their way through the snow packed trees behind the cabin. "We've got to move her."

"I don't know that it will help." Dutch flipped the monitor back around. "I've been checking the footage from our other safe houses." He stopped talking as his fingers flew over two separate sets of keys.

"And?" Wade rounded the desk, unwilling to wait for Dutch's attention to find its way back to him. His gaze moved between the screens. Each showed one of the cabins Alaskan Security used to house clients.

LOSS RECOVERY

Dutch pointed to one as a group of men matching the ones from today appeared on the footage. "That's cabin two." He hit a button on the neighboring laptop. "That's cabin seven."

The same group of five moved across the screen, toward the empty cabin, systematically surrounding the building before one of the men crept up the steps and punched at the keypad.

The air left Wade's lungs. "They're trying to get in."

"They do more than try." Dutch barely glanced up at him before reaching out to stop the playback.

Wade grabbed his outstretched arm, holding firm as the video continued to play. He watched as the man shoved open the door and walked in.

"They knew the code." Wade dropped Dutch's arm as Brock kicked his feet from the table and jumped from his seat.

"What did you say?" He shoved in on the other side of Dutch, eyes narrowing on the screen as the man came out the back door and punched at the pad again. "Did that fucker lock the door behind him?"

"Seems like." Dutch looked from Wade to Brock. "If they have the code to seven—"

"Shit." Wade pulled Parker into his chest and moved from behind the desk. "Shit." He wiped one hand down his face.

"How in the hell did they get the code?" Brock's narrowed gaze turned to Dutch.

"Same way they found all our safe houses." Dutch dropped back into the chair. "They hacked into our system." He pulled one of the laptops closer and started typing again. "They hit the other two cabins right before this one so I haven't had time to try to find how they got in, but if I'm looking for that it means I can't be trying to find out who they fuck they are."

"We need another man on this." The words were barely out of Wade's mouth when Shawn came into the office.

"I've got leads on a few specialists." He flipped out a paper. "You got any preferences?"

Dutch didn't even look up. "The best one."

"Got it." Shawn thumbed across the screen of his phone. "I'll have them here tonight."

"Get him here as fast as you can." Dutch shook his head. "Until then I've got to lock everything down and go offline."

"What's that involve?" Brock stood back as Shawn stepped in to pass Dutch a large insulated cup.

"We've got to manually reset the codes on all the safe houses. Everyone has to ditch their phones and get new trash cells." He pulled the ear piece out of his ear. "I gotta shut these off too. They run through the system."

Brock's gaze met Wade's before moving to Shawn. "How long till we can have that hacker here?"

"Tonight at the earliest."

"And then he has to find how they got in and figure out how to fix it." Dutch shook his head. "We might not be back online for days."

The room went quiet for a minute. Finally Dutch took a deep breath, eyes settling on Wade. "You gotta ask her what the fuck is going on, man. This can't be just a pissed off ex."

"He's a senator's son." The explanation was weak at best. Even a senator's son wouldn't have access to a team like the one they were dealing with. "He thinks Parker is his."

"Is he?" Shawn looked from the little boy to Wade.

Wade shook his head. "No."

Shawn nodded. "The first thing we're doing is getting proof of that. Then we're sending it out to every-fucking-one involved. If by some chance this is her ex, maybe it will calm his tits a little."

"Or it'll piss him off more." Brock propped one ass cheek on the desk beside where Dutch was completely focused on his computers.

"Good." Shawn leaned against the door casing. "Maybe we can push him over the edge. Give us the opportunity to end this the easy way."

Brock's dark eyes moved to Wade. "She know what could happen?"

Wade nodded. "I made it pretty clear."

His partner's gaze didn't waver. "She gonna look at you the same after you kill someone she knows?"

"As long as she's safe she can look at me however she wants." Wade turned to Shawn. "Get me a new phone and get one for Bess." He glanced back at Dutch. "Find out where the fuck Chris is." He was almost out the door when Brock's voice stopped him.

"Find out what this is really about, Wade. It's the only way we might be able to keep her safe."

Wade barely nodded as he walked out of the office.

"I'm not hiding anything."

He jumped back, spinning to find Bess sitting on the ground beside the office door. Her pale brows lifted. "What?"

"Why are you sitting on the floor?"

"Because no one ever looks down." She pushed up from her spot. "Makes it easier to listen without being caught."

"You could have come in."

Bess shook her head. "You were right. They wouldn't have said half of what they did if they knew I was listening." She'd changed out of her pine-needle-littered pajamas and was now in a pair of fitted jeans and a bulky white sweater that seemed to swallow her up. "It has to be Chris." Her hazel eyes searched his. "Right?"

She wanted him to tell her this was a danger she knew. One she was familiar with. One she could anticipate to a certain extent.

But he couldn't lie to her. "How much money does he have at his disposal?"

Bessie's brows came together. "I mean, a decent amount I guess."

"Hundreds of thousands?" Wade stepped closer, feeling like she was too far away. "To spend on punishing you?"

"Hundreds of thousands?" The lines between her brows deepened. "What would—"

"There's someone out there willing to spend that much to have you taken out, Bess."

"Taken out?" Her skin paled.

"Those men weren't shooting at you for fun. They had every intention of hitting you and anyone who got in the way."

"But I was in that big coat. The hood was up. Maybe they thought I was one of you." Her words came faster and faster as she tried to reason what happened away.

He shook his head. "We are trained to be positive before we shoot, Sweetheart. Those men were aiming for you."

"What do you mean, we?" The words were hushed as if she could barely get them out her lips.

"Those men were trained to kill." He took a breath, knowing what he said next could change everything. "Like me."

Her whole body was still, eyes locked onto him. "You would do that?"

"No. We don't take hit jobs." Wade wanted to hold her. Explain all the ways he was different from the men trying to hurt her.

But the truth was the differences were few.

"Is that what you think that was? A hit?" Bess was surprisingly calm considering she was most likely the target of a well-trained team of hit men.

"We're not sure what is going on just yet." Shawn stepped out of the office. "Why don't you come in and see if we can figure out what's going on?" He stepped to one side, letting Bess pass him into the room. Before Wade could follow, Shawn blocked his path. "I think we need to talk to her without you."

"Like hell." Wade grabbed Shawn by the front of his shirt, fisting the fabric tight as he shoved him to one side, only to be blocked again. This time by Brock.

"He's right." Brock reached out to tickle Parker's belly. "Why don't you and little man here go have a snack or something?" Brock pulled the door most of the way closed. "I'll take care of her. I promise. We need her to be honest and she might not tell you the whole truth."

The accuracy of his statement stung.

He and Bess didn't have the best track record when it came to telling each other the truth. "Fine." Wade shoved a finger in his friend's face. "But I swear to God if you upset her I will kick every ass in that room."

"And I thought you were a pain in the ass before." Brock shut the door.

Wade tried to twist the handle.

Locked.

Bastard locked him out.

"You're not getting in until we're done, Wade. Go play with your kid." Brock's voice carried through the wood panel.

Wade glared at the door for a second before Parker started getting restless in his arms.

"Alright, Buddy." Wade carefully set the toddler on his feet. "You wanna run around a little?"

Parker held up one hand, opening and closing his fingers. "Hep."

Wade tucked his pointer and middle finger into Parker's fist. "I'll help you." He walked behind, bent over, as Parker walked toward the kitchen where Tyson, Nate, and Abe were sitting around the island, a line of cells between them. Tyson glanced up. "How's your arm?"

"Fine." It was amazing how easy it was to forget you'd been shot. "What are you doing?"

"Setting up phones." Abe thumbed across the screen of the cell in his hand. "Dutch usually does it, but he's covered up."

Wade grabbed the box of Cheerios off the counter and dumped some into a small plastic bowl before dropping Parker into his high-chair and setting the bowl on the tray. He sat on the stool next to him and grabbed a phone.

Nate slid a sheet of numbers his way. Each was labeled with one of their names. "Program those in. Sounds like we're going old school, so this is all we've got for a while."

"Who's going to reset the codes on the cabins?"

Tyson glanced up from his phone. "We're going out when we're done with this. You comin'?"

Wade glanced at the door, then at Parker. "Maybe."

CHAPTER 10

BESS GLANCED AT the door as it opened. Her heart picked up, expecting to see Wade.

Instead Tyson gave her a small smile when his eyes caught hers. One that looked a little like an apology.

Brock turned his back to her as the two men spoke low enough she couldn't hear anything.

"Are you positive there isn't anything else?"

Shawn was sitting across the large table, elbows leaned on the surface as he stared at her.

Bess pulled her attention from the men at the door. "There's literally nothing else." When she looked back at the door it was shut again and now Brock was gone too.

Leaving her alone with Shawn and Dutch, who hadn't looked up from his computers once in the last hour.

"There has to be something, Bess." It almost seemed like Shawn was pleading with her. "Nothing will leave this room. I swear."

She focused on Shawn. He wasn't bad looking. Tall and broad like the rest of the men filling the cabin, with blond hair and grey eyes. Most women probably fell all over themselves when his attention was focused on them.

Right now it was just pissing her off.

"Are you insinuating something?"

"No." He blew out a breath. "No. I'm just saying you can and should tell me anything that might be relevant."

"I feel like you think I'm hiding something because I don't want Wade to find out." She stared him down.

Shawn leaned closer, his gaze steady. "I think there's a man in the other room who feels pretty sure his whole life changed. If there's a chance it's not true, I need to know."

"Chris doesn't care about Parker outside of the fact that he can use him against me." Bess straightened in her seat. "As far as who Parker's father is, there's a slim chance it is Chris. I've never tried to hide that." She narrowed her eyes on Shawn. "From anyone."

He stared at her for a second before the corners of his mouth twitched. "I read the police reports, Bess."

She crossed her arms over her chest. "So."

Shawn leaned back in his seat. "You jumped onto a moving car to save your son."

Bess lifted one shoulder. "I fell back off."

He nodded slowly. "That didn't stop you though, did it?"

"He had my son." The memory of that day was enough to send her to her feet. "I want Parker. Where is he? Where's Wade?" Bess rounded the table, shoving into Shawn as he tried to block her from leaving. "Get out of my way."

"Parker is fine. He's with Brock." Shawn grabbed her arms.

"Brock?" Why would he be with Brock? Bess spun her arms inward, breaking the grip Shawn had on her. "Where's Wade? He's supposed to be with Wade." She grabbed the door handle and yanked it open. "Wade?"

The cabin was quiet as she rushed into the great room. Brock sat on the floor with Parker, an array of toys scattered around them. He glanced up as she rushed in.

"Where's Wade?" Bess scanned the space as she dropped to pick Parker up, pulling her wiggling son into a hug.

"He'll be back soon." Brock leaned back against the large sectional dominating the space.

She took a breath against Parker's head, trying to soothe the panic building in her stomach. Parker was safe. He was here with her.

Except Parker's safety wasn't the only one she now had to worry about. "Where did he go?"

"He just had a couple errands to run." Brock grabbed the remote off the coffee table and switched on the large-screened television. "He'll be back in a little bit."

"What errands is he running?"

Brock stared at the television. Ignoring her.

"Wade told you to tell me whatever I wanted to know, remember?"

"Shit." Brock dropped his head back to the couch behind him. "I'm gonna kick his ass the next time I see him."

"Liar." She'd heard every man in the house threaten to kick someone's ass in the past twenty-four hours and had yet to see any ass-kicking happen. "Where is he?"

"He's helping reset the codes on the safe houses." Shawn came into the room behind her.

She turned to face Shawn. "Why?"

"Because this is his job, Bess. It's what he does." Shawn stopped just in front of her. His gaze barely flicked to where she clutched Parker to her chest. "And I don't think that's going to change."

She tipped her chin up. "If you think I'm the kind of girl who makes her choices based on what other people think, then you're wrong." Bess shot him one last glare before spinning away and marching into the master bedroom.

She needed some freaking space from the mounds of testosterone bleeding into her life. The slam of the door at her back felt better than it should.

Temper tantrums were ridiculous. They made it look like you didn't have control over yourself or your life.

But right now she didn't seem to have too much of either.

"I think your mommy's going a little crazy, Park." Bess stretched her little boy across the bed and went to work changing his diaper. It was a simple act, but one that had always been oddly soothing. Taking care of Parker was what got her through this past year. All her attention went to him. To his needs.

It kept her from thinking about her own.

About how alone she felt. How alone she was.

"Damn it." Bess swiped her forearm under her nose.

Shawn might be right.

It was the reason Wade claimed he left her that night. Maybe he liked this life. Liked the rush he must get every time he did something like what he was doing now.

Maybe his whole plan was to do his job and move on. Prove Chris wasn't Parker's father. Right the chaos of her life.

And then disappear.

Again.

****

BESS SAT UPRIGHT in the bed, jerking awake in an instant. It only took a second to register the form of a man looming over the bed where she and Parker fell asleep. She grabbed Parker and rolled away from the man reaching for her, trying to get her son as far from his reach as she could.

"Bess, it's me." Wade grabbed her just as her body started to slide off the side of the mattress. He dragged her back across the bed, pulling her and

Parker closer. "Be careful. You're going to wake him up." Wade's voice was soft. "Brock said he just fell asleep." One large hand settled onto Parker's back, pausing a second before sliding up to rest against his head. "He feels hot."

"I think he's getting more teeth." Bess had walked the floor with Parker, his fussiness working as a convenient excuse to pace, as she waited for Wade to come back. "Where were you?"

Wade's hand moved from Parker to her, brushing the hair off her face with a gentle touch. Would he touch her like that if his intention was to let her go again?

Maybe.

"We had to reset all the codes on our cabins manually. I went with the team that did it so I could see if there was anything that might help us figure out who is involved in this besides Chris." Wade eased down beside her, his movement sending the damp scent of fresh soap into the air between them. "This isn't Chris, Bess."

"It is." They didn't know her. She understood that, but in her whole life she'd only had one enemy.

One.

And so far he'd held her against her will, kidnapped her son, assaulted her, and stalked her. "It has to be him."

Wade's hand curved against the side of her face. "I'm not saying I think Chris is innocent." He scooted a little closer, pulling her against him with Parker tucked safely between their bodies. "But

134

there is more to this than a pissed off senator's son."

An odd sensation bubbled its way through her, sneaking up and out.

"Bess. Why are you laughing? I'm serious."

"Because it's ridiculous. You're saying there's not just one, but two people who want to kill me." Bess wiped at one eye as it started to water. "I'm nobody. I'm some chick who lives in Oregon and works for her parents. I don't go out. I don't socialize. You can count the people who know me on your fingers."

And how freaking depressing was that? Her night with Wade was the most exciting thing she'd ever done. The biggest risk she'd ever taken.

"Maybe it's not about you then." There was something off in Wade's tone. He shifted off the bed. He pressed a kiss to her lips. "Go back to sleep."

And then he was gone.

A-freaking-gain.

Whatever. She'd been alone for two years and would have been just fine if Chris hadn't gone crazy.

She could be alone again.

It would be just fine.

Bess curled around her sleeping son's little body, resting her lips against his sweaty head. If Wade wanted to fix this mess and then go on his way then so be it.

She was a big girl. She would handle it.

A minute later the door to her room opened.

And he was back again.

"Go away, Wade." The way the demand made her feel was an issue she would save for another day. Right now she had to find a place to keep her sanity. Her clarity.

Because since the second Wade walked into the cabin, deep down she'd been sure everything was coming full-circle.

That their paths were crossing again for a reason.

Fate.

Which was silly. Stupid, actually.

Because at the end of the day, they'd spent one single night together two years ago. That was it.

Nothing more.

And while Wade claimed it was more than that, maybe it was more about guilt.

Or worse.

Regret.

"Bess?" He came closer, completely ignoring her request. "What's wrong, Sweetheart?"

"Don't call me that." She held Parker tighter. "Just go. Please."

"No."

The single word sent her sitting up and spinning to face him. "No?"

"That's what I said." Wade kept coming closer, stopping right next to the bed before leaning down, one hand pushed into the mattress on each side of her. "Seems like you heard me." His face dropped close to hers. "Why don't you tell me what's wrong?"

Bess swallowed down the urge to tell him. Spill out all the silly dreams she'd been holding close since the night they met.

That if he only knew he would come back. Would wish he'd never left.

And in some ways that was true. Wade would have come back. He did wish he never left.

It never occurred to her that he would leave again, though. "This isn't going to go anywhere, Wade."

He was so still. So silent. The sound of his breathing, and her heart pounding was all there was.

"Bess."

"What."

"I'm not leaving you again." He eased closer, his big body crowding hers back. "Eventually you will figure that out."

"You left me today." The bit she'd hoped to keep jumped free, showing Wade a bit of the fear she didn't want to have.

Because who was scared to lose a man they didn't really know? A man they spent one night with?

"I will do whatever it takes to keep you and Parker safe, Bess. Today that meant I had to leave you for a few hours." His nose slid alongside hers. "But I came back. I always will."

"For Parker."

"We covered this, Sweetheart. I feel like I explained it pretty well, but obviously you're still unclear." Wade shifted away, taking the solid sense of safety she only felt when he was close.

And son of a bitch she whimpered when it happened.

"I'm right here." His hands moved from the bed to her body, warm and steady as they rested against her hips. His lips brushed over her neck, drifting down until they caught on the neck of her shirt. He breathed deep, his exhale hot against her skin. "I fucking missed you."

"You were only gone a few hours." Her eyes slipped shut as his hands slid up her ribcage, dragging the fabric of her shirt along with it.

"I'm not talking about just today." His thumbs stroked over her skin. "I missed you every damn day for the past two years." Wade took another breath against her body. "Missed the way you smell." His lips nipped the skin at the crook of her neck. "Missed the way you taste. Missed everything about you."

"You don't know everything about me." Bess rested her hands on his shoulders, intending to push him away. "You don't really know anything about me."

"I know more than you think." Wade's arms wrapped around her back, pulling her toward the edge of the bed. "I know you're the best fucking mother I've ever seen."

Her body scooted again, edging closer to him.

"I know you don't back down from anyone."

He pulled again and her legs fell over the edge of the bed.

"I know you are more sensitive than you want people to know." He leaned into her. "I know you over think the shit out of everything."

"Not everything."

His head bobbed in the darkness as he nodded at her. "Everything."

"I just like to be prepared for anything."

"Is that why you're sure I'm going to disappear again? So you'll be ready?" His hands pressed into her back, holding her body close to his. It's one of the many things she'd imagined in those silent, solitary moments. Wade holding her close. Making her feel safe.

Protected.

"Yes."

His head lifted, eyes lining up with hers. "I know you don't believe it. I get that. I deserve to not be trusted—"

"I trust you." This had nothing to do with trust. This had to do with reality.

The shadow of his lips curved into an easy smile. "Then trust me."

"But—"

"Bess." Wade's hands came up to each side of her face. "You don't have to believe me, just trust me."

She nodded, a knot of emotion tying up any hope of forming words.

His lips brushed over hers. Once.

Twice.

The third pass of his mouth was different, slower, firmer. Deeper.

His tongue teased hers as his hands pushed into her hair, tangling in the strands.

Two years ago Wade gave her the best, most physically satisfying night of her life. A night she'd reflected on an embarrassing number of times. Usually with the company of a vibrator.

But now the real thing was right in front of her again. Saying all the right things. Helping with Parker. Saving her life.

At every turn Wade was showing her he was capable of being more than just a bedroom companion.

And maybe she should believe him. Maybe he wouldn't leave.

Maybe this could be all that she'd let herself imagine it could be.

"I want you, Wade." Bess pushed into him, knocking him back a little and sending him off balance.

His arms held her tight as they both went down to the ground, him taking the brunt of the impact, being careful no part of her hit with any sort of force. She tried to pull him close, fighting for some leverage with a man who was significantly taller than she was.

"Hang on, Sweetheart." Wade rolled her to one side, away from the bed.

"Hang on? It's been two freaking years since I've gotten laid." Not the most ladylike way to put things, but she was feeling a little desperate and a lot ready to have a repeat of their one night together.

Wade chuckled low in the darkness. "Have I said you are impatient yet?" One big hand wrapped around the back of her head, pulling her in for a mind-numbing kiss before breaking free

140

and rolling away. A sound similar to a drawer being opened cut through the quiet room.

And then she was against him again, held tight as Wade barely lifted her off the ground and eased her body onto a bed. A floor bed.

Bess rolled her head from one side to the other, trying to get her bearings in the almost completely dark room. "Is this another mattress?"

"It's a trundle bed." Wade's big body hovered over her, smothering out what little light the tiny bulb in the outlet across the room provided. "Slides out from under the bed."

"That's convenient."

"I thought so." A little of his weight pressed onto her. "We don't have to rush this, Bess."

"We've already had sex. I'm not sure what we would be rushing." She gripped his shirt, desperation making her a little more aggressive than normal. "And it's been two freaking years. I need this."

Wade stilled. "If you just need to get off, then I'm happy to help, but I'm not fucking you until I know you're ready."

"You already fucked me." Was this a crazy conversation? It felt like a crazy conversation. She wanted to have sex. They had already had sex. What was the issue?

"I fucked you then because you knew what it was." Wade's hands pushed her shirt up again, this time taking it all the way off. "I'm not sure you're ready for what it is now."

Any questions she might have had about the differences between sex two years ago and sex tonight were forgotten when his mouth caught her nipple, hot and strong.

A part of her had been worried she would feel differently about this particular act now that she'd breast fed.

Nope.

His mouth moved from one breast to the other, sucking and licking each tip until Bess was pretty sure she was going to murder him for refusing to have sex this very second.

Then one hand tugged down the plaid pajama bottoms she wore, taking panties and all. Wade eased down her body, nipping at the lined skin of her belly before settling between her thighs. His fingers slid along her slit, gliding over her clit with a barely-there touch before easing into her body, stroking with a maddeningly slow touch.

One that would never get her where she wanted to go.

Bess pushed against him, trying to speed the process up. Speed him up.

Wade's laugh came low and close.

"Definitely impatient."

CHAPTER 11

"I'M NOT IMPATIENT, you're just frustrating."

Bess might be glaring at him, but the lust in her eyes said she wasn't as upset as she pretended to be. "I don't remember you being frustrated two years ago."

"Two years ago you moved a whole lot faster."

Wade smiled up at her. "Two years ago I was on a schedule." He nipped the inside of one thigh as he continued teasing her with his fingers. "Now I have all the time in the world."

She gasped as his lips worked closer to her pussy. "That's not true. There's a baby who could wake up any second three feet away and I swear to God I will kill you if that happens."

He blew out a breath, focusing the stream of air on her clit. Bessie's soft moan barely reached his ears as her hand fisted in his hair. "That's new."

"Not new, Sweetheart. You've only had a tiny taste of the things I plan to do to you." He caught her legs and spread them wide. "And I plan to take my time and enjoy every fucking second of it."

Two years of suffering, fighting himself every day, it all felt worth it in this moment.

Bess was here. The only woman to ever make him second guess the choices he'd made in his life.

And this time she didn't come alone. That meant this time he had every reason in the world to do exactly what he wanted.

Keep her.

Take care of her.

Do what he should have done the first time.

Wade skimmed his hands up her thighs, over the soft line of her hips, hating the jut of bone pushing up.

She hadn't been taking care of herself, that was for damn sure. He hated the dark hint of shadows under her eyes. The way her frame was thinner in spite of carrying a baby. The anxiety he watched her fight anytime Parker was out of her sight.

He would get to work fixing all of that just as soon as he gave her what she needed this minute.

"Remember when I asked who you thought of when you touched yourself?" His lips barely brushed across her pubic bone as he spoke.

"Yes." The word was ragged as his tongue slid down the center of her.

"Do you want to know what I thought of?"

Her head tipped up, hazel eyes meeting his. "Yes."

144

"This." His tongue probed deeper, slipping between her labia to tease over the hard nub of her clit. "I fucked my hand while I thought of you coming on my tongue."

Her lips barely parted, the tip of her tongue sliding over them as she watched him. "Do it then."

Wade's eyes locked onto hers. "Sweetheart, you might be more than I can handle."

"Probably." Bess rubbed her lips together as they pressed into a sly little smile. "I'll let you try to do it anyway."

"That's nice of you." Wade leaned in, ready to show her just how much effort he intended to put into his attempt, but Bess scooted away.

"I thought you were going to—" Her eyes darted to the athletic pants he put on after taking the fastest shower in history. "Multitask."

She was serious. "You want me to jack off while I lick your pussy?"

Bess nodded. "I do."

Fuck. She really might be more than he could handle.

"Unless you would rather just have sex." That sly smile was back.

"You're a fucking minx, you know that?" Wade pushed up to his knees. "Sneaky little siren."

Bess lifted one shoulder. "I just wanted to give you options. Maybe tempt you to change your mind."

He tugged the back of his t-shirt with one hand, pulling the garment up and off before shoving his pants down just far enough to release his dick, which was entirely on board with Bessie's primary objective.

It was going to have to fucking wait too.

Because he'd screwed this up with her once. It wasn't happening again.

"Give me a little credit as a man." Wade dropped over her, catching himself with both hands. "I have *some* willpower."

"How much?" One hand slid down her body. "Exactly?"

Wade caught her wrist, stopping the wayward hand just as it found the spot he intended to own. "Not that much."

Wade lifted her fingers to his mouth and pulled them between his lips, sucking the barely-there taste of her off before letting them fall free. Bess watched with wide eyes, not blinking until he pressed her hand into the bed at her side. He eased back into his place, shifting her legs wider with his shoulders as he rested on one side.

He took himself in hand as his mouth went to work, finding a rhythm that seemed to be working for both of them. Bess had one hand in his hair and used the other to hold herself up, heavy-lidded gaze bouncing from where his mouth worked to where his fist did.

"That is so hot." It came out on a pant, her fingers tightening against his scalp.

She gasped as he sucked her clit. "Wade."

He groaned a little at the sound of his name in her voice, full of need and lust. His cock twitched against his palm, fighting for the chance to release. He held back, even as her thighs shook against him and her clit hardened to a bead under his tongue. No one came first but her.

Bess pushed up higher, the hand in his hair pulling harder, shoving his mouth tight against her as she ground against his face.

It was one of the things that struck him most that night. How unashamed she was of her own desires, her own wants. So many women seemed to hold back for whatever reason, and he loved that she didn't.

But right now it was making his life hell.

Because every breath she took, every move she made, every sound that slipped through her lips, was threatening to sever the rein he had on his climax.

The second her hips bucked and her legs tensed relief flooded through him. She came holding his head against her, eyes locked onto where he stroked his almost painfully erect dick. Bess watched as his balls pulled up tight, his orgasm ripping through him a second later, spilling into the fabric of the shirt he shucked.

"Oh my God." Her hand left his hair to mash into her own, pushing the strands back and up. "That was…"

Wade grabbed the soiled shirt and bunched it up into a wad before pulling the waistband of his pants back into place.

"I don't even know what that was." Bess blinked long and slow, her eyes coming back into focus as he crawled over her. "You make me act crazy."

Wade lifted his brows. "I make you act crazy?"

The flush on her cheeks deepened. "I'm not usually that..." She chewed her lower lip for a second. "Forward."

He leaned into her soft body. "That's a shame. A woman who knows what she wants is a beautiful thing." He nuzzled her neck, pressing her down to the mattress of the trundle bed. "You can boss me around in the bedroom anytime you want."

"In that case—"

"Not fucking you yet, Sweetheart."

Bess huffed out a breath that had him laughing as he collected her pajamas from beside them. "Pout about it all you want. It won't change my mind." He righted her shirt and pulled it over her head, covering up the body he couldn't wait to fully explore.

"What will change your mind?"

Wade eased her pants over each foot and up her legs. "Start getting enough sleep and eating right and maybe I'll consider it."

"That's blackmail."

He smiled, pulling her up from the trundle and shoving it back into place with his foot before easing her onto the mattress beside where Parker was still sleeping soundly.

"Whatever it takes, Sweetheart." He brushed a kiss over her lips. "No more putting yourself last."

She scoffed. "I had other things to worry about."

"And now they're my things to worry about." He slid under the covers beside her. "All you have to do is let me take care of you."

Bess pursed her lips, staring at him for a second.

"I'll think about it."

****

"IT'S TIME TO get up, Sweetheart." Wade leaned closer to the woman still tucked into bed, sleeping soundly.

Hopefully he had something to do with that.

She barely stirred, a long deep breath making it appear Bess wasn't any closer to waking up then when he forced himself out from beside her to go check in with Dutch. The hacker should be here any minute and Wade wanted to fill Bess in on what he found out before another person descended on the cabin.

He kneeled on the floor, somehow managing to avoid the temptation to lie back beside her. "Bess. I need you to wake up."

Her lids lifted, revealing hazel eyes still clouded and groggy. She smiled, slow and sleepy. "Hey."

It was the first time he'd seen her wake up without immediately reaching to be sure Parker was okay.

Hopefully he had something to do with that too. "Good morning."

Her gaze moved to the window beside the bed. "Is it morning?"

"It is." Wade reached out to run his fingers through the tangled strands of her hair. "Sun doesn't come up until almost lunchtime, remember?"

Her nose wrinkled. "Is that hard to get used to?"

He shrugged. "The snow helps. Makes it seem brighter than it is."

Bess studied him for a minute. "Where did you grow up?"

He felt like he knew so much about her. Who she really was. What was important to her. How far she would go to protect what mattered to her.

Hopefully she knew the same sort of things about him.

But they hadn't covered the basics most people start with.

"Missouri."

"Branson?"

A bark of laughter caught him by surprise. How long had it been since he'd really laughed?

Fucking forever.

"No. Definitely not Branson."

Bessie's smile widened. "I feel like you probably never even gave it a chance."

Wade laced the fingers of one hand with hers. "Maybe we can go there when this is all over. Make Missouri your second trip out of Oregon."

Her smile faded. "I can't believe you remembered."

"That you've never been outside of Oregon?" Wade stroked her thumb with his. "Until now." His movement stopped. "Was that your first plane trip?"

Bess nodded.

Her first plane trip was with a baby. Alone. On the run.

150

Wade rested his forehead against hers. "I'm going to make all this up to you, Bess. I promise."

"Maybe I'll let you try later." Her voice carried a smile.

"I won't waste the opportunity." He wanted to start now. Crawl back into her bed and give her what he held back last night.

But it still wasn't right. Not yet.

"I have someone coming today." He leaned back so he could look into her eyes. "To see Parker."

Bess barely nodded as her lips rolled together.

"It doesn't change anything, Bess. No matter what." He stroked across her cheek. "I will take care of both of you no matter what the test says."

"I know." Her whisper was almost lost on the shift of air as the front door opened. Bess glanced over his shoulder, her hands reaching for him as she started to sit up.

Because she knew he would protect her from whatever might be coming. But this time there was no threat.

Hopefully the opposite.

"That's the hacker coming to help Dutch figure out who got into our system and how they did it." He pushed up from the floor, dreading the next bit he had to tell her. "I have to leave for a little while today after the woman comes to collect my sample."

Bess nodded. "Okay."

"But Dutch will be here and so will Shawn and Nate. You and Parker will be safe."

"What about you?" Bessie's eyes were rimmed with unease as she stared up at him. "Will you be safe?"

"I'm not planning on getting shot twice in one week, Sweetheart." Wade pulled her into his arms, holding her close. "I said I wasn't leaving you again and I meant it. Come hell or high water I will always come back to you, understand?"

There was a knock on the bedroom door a second before it cracked open. Brock peeked through the small opening. "You decent?"

Wade leaned into Bessie's ear. "When this is all over I'm taking you someplace where you can be as alone as you want to be, I promise."

"You're making an awful lot of promises." She was soft in his arms. Relaxed in spite of all that was happening.

"I'm trying to give you plenty of reasons to keep me around."

Her head tipped to one side. "Is that what you want? Me to keep you around?"

"Sweetheart, if you hadn't already figured that out then I'm not sure there's much I can tell you to make you believe it." He caught her mouth in a quick kiss. "You'll figure it out eventually though."

"Dude, I know you've got shit to work out, but I need help out here." Brock turned to glance over his shoulder. "I think someone's going to die."

Bess went still.

Brock's eyes widened. "Parker's fine. He's happy as hell hanging out with Tyson." The sound of shouting drifted in through the crack in the door.

"Dutch might not make it through the day though."

Wade started across the room, barely making it two steps before Bessie's hand was sliding into his. She followed close beside him, wary gaze locked on the spot where Brock stood. The yelling grew louder with each step they took, but it wasn't until they were almost to the door that Wade realized who was raising hell in the great room.

He pulled the door open just as a tiny woman in thick black glasses shoved her finger into the middle of Dutch's chest with enough force it would definitely leave a bruise. "It doesn't take a sack to do this shit, dick."

Dutch was sputtering, eyes wide. Probably from fear, because the tiny woman's size appeared to be the only thing small about her. Her voice picked up as she continued on. "I'm sorry I don't have the knob you were hoping for."

"No one said they were hoping you had a..." Shawn glanced around the roomful of men, probably looking for help.

"Knob." Bess finished for him. She smiled at the small, dark-haired hellion who somehow managed to have more than a few men ready to tuck tail and run in the less than five minutes she'd been in their presence. "I'm Bess." She dropped Wade's hand and crossed the room to where the other woman stood, head high, spine straight. Still ready to do battle with anyone who crossed her.

She was exactly what they needed.

The woman shoved her hand into Bessie's. "Harlow Mowry." She glanced Dutch's way. "The dickless hacker you all spent a shit load of money flying in from New York."

"Rumor has it you're the best." Shawn edged in a little closer, his bravery resurfacing now that Bess was between him and Harlow.

"It's not a rumor." Harlow grabbed the handle to the black rolling suitcase at her side. "So am I staying or are you going to find the second-best hacker?" Her blue eyes moved to Dutch. "That one has a penis."

"I didn't say I wanted a hacker with a penis." Dutch ran one hand through his already messy dark hair. The guy had been up all night trying to find the break in their system and it showed. He had bags under his eyes and the line of his jaw was heavily shadowed with stubble.

Harlow stepped around Bess, clearly not noticing the exhausted state of the man she was going to war with. Or maybe she just didn't care. "You said 'you're a woman'. Same fucking thing."

Dutch shoved one finger in Harlow's direction. "You know damn well most hackers are men. Don't even pretend like I should have expected you to be a woman."

"It shouldn't matter what I am." Harlow glared at Dutch, propping her hand on her jean-clad hip. "It should only matter what I can do."

Wade stepped between Harlow and Dutch, turning to face the woman who made Bess look tall. This situation had to be diffused and it had to be done now. They needed Harlow working, not fighting. He held his hand out to her. "I'm Wade."

She eyed his hand for a heartbeat before taking it with a grip he saw coming. "Are you an ass too?"

"Sometimes." He tipped his head toward the exhausted man at his back. "He's been up all night trying to figure this out. We need you. Are you willing to stay?"

Harlow eyed Dutch over Wade's shoulder. "Hell yeah, I'm staying. This job pays me as much as I made last year." She tipped her bag down onto its rollers and pointed toward the office. "Am I setting up in there?"

"You can set up wherever you want." Wade stepped aside as she started walking.

Marching maybe. Her walk was proud and purposeful as she breezed past Dutch, head turning to stare him down as she went.

Bess stepped in beside him as Harlow disappeared into the office. "She's bad-ass."

Wade nodded.

"Yes she is."

CHAPTER 12

BESS EYED THE woman from the lab as she swabbed Parker's cheek.

Parker's brows were together, low over the almost black eyes glaring at the woman as she wiggled the plastic-tipped wand around his mouth.

Wade stepped in, resting one hand on the little boy's back. "She's almost done, Buddy."

Parker's little mouth tipped into a frown and his eyes watered.

But he didn't cry.

"That's it. Be brave." Wade rubbed in a circle over the fuzzy sleeper Parker was wearing.

The woman pulled the swab free and tucked it into a labeled tube. "All done." She smiled at Parker. "You did a good job." Her gaze lifted to Wade, narrowing for just a second before moving to Parker and then back again. "Is this just a formality?" Her eyes went to Parker again. "Because he looks just like you."

Bess was still considering taking a trip to the bathroom to puke, but somehow managed a small smile. "I think so too."

The woman gave her a nod as she packed up the tubes and collected the wrappers. "They should have results for you in the next 24 hours."

"That fast?" Her stomach rolled.

The woman smiled brightly. "Right?" She tickled Parker's belly. "Fastest in the nation." Her smile lifted even more when Rico edged in at her side.

"All finished?" Rico barely glanced Bessie's way as he directed the woman from the lab toward the door, ushering her out to the black SUV waiting in the driveway to take her back to work.

"That's it then." Bess stared at the door as it closed behind them. "By tomorrow we'll know for sure."

"We will." Wade pulled her close. "It's going to be okay, Bess. I promise."

"You keep saying that, but I'm not sure that's something you have control over." Her eyes lifted to his. "He's not going to be happy if he's not Parker's father."

"When." He tipped her chin higher with the press of a finger. "He won't be happy when we have proof he's not Parker's father."

She tried to breathe deep, force the air into her burning lungs, but it was almost impossible. "I hope so."

Wade's lips twisted before curving into a smile. "Stubborn."

Bess blew out the air she'd worked so hard to get in. "I'm not stubborn. I'm trying to be realistic."

"If you were being realistic, then you would have taken one look at him and realized who he belonged to." Wade's head tilted, eyes narrowing for a second. "Maybe that's why he's so pissed."

Bess widened her eyes, waiting for an explanation. "Why?"

Wade brushed the shock of dark hair off Parker's forehead. "Because he already knows Parker isn't his."

Parker fell forward into Wade's waiting arms. He swept him high into the air. "Everyone knows but your momma, Buddy." He shot her a wink. "She's being stubborn."

"I'm not stubborn."

"Why not?"

Bess turned to find Harlow standing behind her, sucking down a cup of coffee. She emptied the cup before sliding it across the counter toward where Nate stood beside the maker. "Fill me up." Her attention turned back to Bess. "Stubborn isn't a bad thing."

Bess tapped one finger on the counter, studying the woman in front of her. She was even shorter than Bess was. It was difficult to tell much else because Harlow was decked out in baggy clothes that hid any hint of her form. Her long dark hair fell in nearly perfect spiral curls that were barely starting to fly away, probably from a long night of travel and then a less than smooth arrival. "Sometimes it is."

Harlow shrugged, a wicked smile showing off the perfect line of her teeth. "But it's still fun."

Bess couldn't help but smile back at her. "I like you."

Harlow gave her a once over. "I like you too."

There were very few people Bess felt comfortable around. Even fewer that she liked.

And Harlow might be both. Probably because she was real. Didn't pretend to be something she wasn't.

At least that's how it seemed so far, but if there was anything she'd learned over the past two years, it was that sometimes people were really good at hiding what they actually were.

Harlow's blue eyes studied Bess for a minute longer, stopping when Nate nudged her elbow with the cup she pushed his way. She took it, that shrewd gaze focusing on him until he backed away, slowly retreating from the kitchen to disappear down the hall.

Harlow sipped at her coffee. "I make men uncomfortable."

"Pretty sure you do it on purpose." Wade moved into the kitchen, pouring some of the coffee into a mug.

"Not always." Harlow huffed out a breath, turning to fully face Bess. "It's going to happen anyway, so occasionally I help expedite the process."

"It's not always going to happen." Bess scooted her butt onto one of the chairs around the island.

160

Harlow pointed one finger at her. "See, that's where you're wrong. It literally happens every time."

Bess glanced at Wade. "It does until it doesn't." She gave Harlow a little smile. "I know what you're saying though."

Bessie's reserved tendencies meant she was regularly passed over in favor of women who were friendlier. Sweeter. More open. Maybe it's why she was with Chris for so long. The idea of finding someone else felt so daunting.

And for a long time she thought a life with Chris would be good enough.

Fine.

Harlow huffed, leaning against the counter. "Men don't like women who are smarter than they are."

"Not true."

Harlow lifted a brow at Wade. "Bullshit."

Bess smiled. Yeah. This chick definitely wasn't the kind to fake anything.

Wade moved in behind Bess. "Men love women who are smarter than they are, but are scared shitless those women are too smart to catch."

Harlow tipped her head Bessie's way. "You caught her."

Wade smiled. "Sure did." He shifted Parker onto her lap and pressed a kiss to her cheek. "I've got to run some errands. I'll be back in a few hours."

Bess held her son close. "You're not going anywhere alone, are you?"

Wade's smile deepened. "Not today. Brock's going with me." He kissed her forehead. "Shawn, Dutch, and Nate are all here, so you girls will be safe."

Harlow lifted a brow.

Wade held up one hand. "Don't start with me, Mowry." He stepped back. "You can lecture me about sexism later."

Harlow's lips pressed together in a hidden smile that she didn't let loose until Wade was well out of sight. "I think I like him too."

"Yup." Bess caught Parker as he started to slide off her lap, trying to get to the floor. "He's turning out to be really likable."

Harlow's dark brows came together. "Isn't he your kid's dad?"

Bess watched as Parker shuffled across the floor toward the center of the great room where a pile of unfamiliar toys were scattered across the carpet. "Hopefully."

Harlow scooted her butt onto the stool beside Bess. "That sounds like an interesting story."

"Interesting isn't the word I would use for it." She cringed as Parker narrowly missed knocking his head on the coffee table as he sat to play. "I would say crazy."

Harlow sipped at her coffee. "You'll have to tell me the whole story."

"Hey." Dutch stormed out of the office looking twice as tired as he did this morning when he and Harlow had it out. "We're paying you a shit ton of money to work."

Harlow didn't turn around. She didn't actually react at all. Just took another sip of her coffee. She leaned back in her chair. "I could tell him I've got a program running right now that will find how the system was breached." She took another drink. "But I don't feel like fucking talking to him."

"I can hear you, Harlow." Dutch moved in at her side. "And I'd like you a lot better if you weren't so fucking condescending."

Harlow finally looked Dutch's way. "I don't give a shit if you like me."

"That's clear." He stepped in close, leaning down until he and Harlow were eye to eye. "But until this is handled I'm your fucking boss, so you sure as shit should try to at least pretend to tolerate me."

"You're not my boss." For the first time Bess saw a crack in Harlow's cool temperament.

And from the look of it Dutch caught it too. He barely smiled. "I definitely am." He rested one hand on the counter at each side of Harlow. "And if you want your full paycheck, then you'll adjust your fucking attitude and try to be a little more pleasant."

Harlow's head tipped to one side. "I have been being pleasant." She returned his smile. "You should see me when I'm being a bitch."

Dutch's eyes barely dropped to Harlow's smile. "I'd like to see that someday." He straightened. "But right now you're the only one here smart enough to figure out who's trying to kill Bess, and if we don't keep her very much alive, Wade is going to murder all of us."

Harlow's blue gaze rested on Bess. "The hackers are after you?" She shook her head a little. "I thought you were just here because you're with Wade."

"I told you it was a crazy story." Bess managed a small smile in spite of the recent reminder of the reality of her current situation.

Harlow studied her for a minute. "Can I read your file?"

"Of course. I'm not sure it will be much help though." Bess stood up as Parker managed to climb onto the coffee table and stand up in the center. She reached him just as he started to tip back, catching him before he could fall. "I'm not sure I agree with everyone else."

"You don't think they're after you?" Harlow was on her feet, lifting her brows and hands at Dutch. "The file?"

Dutch spun away toward the office, shaking his head.

"I don't see how it could be possible." Bess carried Parker back to the kitchen and snagged a container of his favorite snacks from the counter, glancing at the brand new package.

Dutch slapped a large file into Harlow's waiting hands. She immediately flipped it open on the counter and started scanning the pages. "He kidnapped your kid?" Her eyes were wide. "That's more than crazy." She flipped to the next page. "That's psycho."

Bess worked Parker into the high-chair and peeled back the foil from the container of puffs, dropping a few onto the tray. "Yeah, but—"

"Holy shit." Harlow's head snapped up. "They tried to shoot you?"

"I'm not convinced they meant to shoot me specifically." Bess wiped at a smear of cheese powder dusting Parker's cheek.

Harlow was already back to scanning the pages of the file, lips pressed tightly together as she flipped one after the next. Bess tried to focus on Parker the same way she had since he'd been born. Anytime things got to be more than she could handle, she would think of him.

What she was willing to do to keep him safe.

And then she would do it.

It was the only way she could keep moving. Keep functioning.

"You thirsty?" Bess found one of his cups in the dishwasher and filled it with water. He took it as soon as she held it out and sucked down half.

"You might be right." Harlow shoved up from her seat at the island, flipping the file closed, grabbing it with one hand and her coffee with the other. "Come on."

Bess stared after her as Harlow rushed toward the office. She turned in the doorway. "Bring Parker. We'll make one of the boys play with him, but I need you to fill me in."

"Okay." Bess lifted Parker out of his chair and snagged his container of snacks and sippy cup before following Harlow into the office. Dutch sat at the desk, staring between the screens of multiple laptops. Shawn was sitting at the large conference-style table in front of his own laptop, surrounded by papers and open files.

Harlow dropped into a chair at the opposite end where a small computer was set up with a separate, strange-looking keyboard and mouse in front of it. She pulled a chair in close and patted the seat. "Come."

Bess lowered into the chair, watching as Harlow flipped through screens at the speed of light, her pale eyes scanning the different windows as they zipped by. Suddenly the screen went black except for a line of nonsense flashing across the very top.

"The program found where they got in." Harlow's fingers flew over the odd keyboard, bouncing between it and the mouse beside it. Her eyes narrowed on the screen. "That's not good."

Dutch was on his feet, crossing the room. "What?"

Harlow looked at him over the top of her screen. "This isn't just a breech."

Dutch slowed. "No."

Her eyes narrowed and her head dropped to one side. "You didn't think it was a good idea to tell me they also decoded your encryption?"

"You're still on a need-to-know basis."

Harlow's lip curled and one finger pointed Bessie's way. "This woman is being shot at and you have me on a need-to-know basis?" She pushed up out of her chair. "You need to pop your head out of your ass and consider maybe this isn't something to dick around with."

Bess stood up beside Harlow. "You didn't tell her everything she needed to know?"

She had spent every waking minute of the past thirteen months doing whatever had to be done to keep her son safe. Did things no mother should ever have to do.

Stayed awake all night, scared out of her mind that tomorrow would be the day she failed.

And now she might, only it wouldn't be her fault.

Bess didn't think. Didn't even take a breath before picking up the closest thing and chucking it at Dutch.

The sippy cup caught him right between the eyes, bouncing off his forehead before clattering to the ground.

Harlow turned to her. "You're awesome."

Bess nodded. "You too."

Shawn was on his feet, grabbing the container of toddler puffs before she could. "Calm down." He held one hand up. "I'm the one who made that call."

Harlow had her still-full coffee cup in one hand, pulled back just as Dutch caught her wrist. "We didn't know if we could trust you with all the information." He worked the ceramic mug free of her clenched fingers. "We don't take sharing our client's information lightly."

Harlow shook her head at him. "Don't bullshit me, man." She snatched her wrist free of his hold. "It was a test." She turned to Bess. "They wanted to be sure the girl could do what she said she could."

"We would have done the same thing to a man." Shawn sat back in his seat, attention still on

167

Harlow. "You get that chip off your shoulder and I might consider asking you to move to Alaska."

Harlow scrunched her nose at him. "Lucky me." She heaved out a loud sigh. "Anything else I need to know?" She glared at Dutch. "Or am I still outside the circle of trust?"

Dutch rubbed his forehead as he walked back to his desk of computers. "I will send you everything I have as soon as you are sure the firewall is back in place."

"It's already back in place." Harlow said it like anyone with a lick of common sense would have known that already. "That was the first thing I did."

Dutch took a long slow breath and Bess could almost hear him count to ten. "That's great and wonderful news that would have been helpful to have had hours ago."

Harlow smiled. "You should have been able to figure that one out yourself, *boss*." She danced her fingers across the keys of her board. "I'm waiting for that information you're supposed to be sending me."

Bess leaned in, watching as Harlow pulled up a search bar and typed in the name to the county where she lived in Oregon, easily navigating through the tabs to find the Clerk of Courts. In seconds she was pulling up scanned copies of every document she and Chris had filed.

"This dude really wants to piss you off, doesn't he?" Harlow held her coffee with one hand as she continued to type with the other. "He gonna lose his shit when you have proof the kid's not his?"

"His shit was lost a long time ago."

Harlow opened up a window and in a few clicks of her mouse, Chris' Facebook profile opened. She tipped her head to one side, eyes narrowing on the photo of him displayed at the top of the page. "Probably happened the second he saw Parker." She glanced down at where Parker was crawling around under the table. "Were you with him when you got pregnant?"

Bess shook her head. "I'd just told him I didn't want to be with him anymore."

Harlow's head turned toward her. "Did he believe you?"

"Not really."

"Shit." Shawn swore under his breath, catching both women's attention.

"Something wrong?" Harlow leaned back in her chair, coffee cup clutched in one hand.

His cheeks puffed as he blew out a breath between tight lips. Finally he looked at Bess.

"A warrant's been issued for your arrest."

CHAPTER 13

"WE GOT A couple problems."

Wade squinted down at the row of boxes lining the shelf in the small pharmacy. He tucked his cell against his shoulder and reached for one, flipping it over so he could read the directions on the back. "What's wrong?"

He'd known Dutch long enough to be able to tell when something was really wrong, and when Dutch was just blowing shit out of proportion.

"Your girl's got a warrant." The sound of Dutch's fingers on the keyboard in the background was a good sign.

"I'm assuming you're on it?"

"As on it as I can be with the other problem."

"What's the other problem?" Wade added the box to the basket slung over his arm then tossed in a few more options just in case.

"Your girl and Harlow are fucking best friends already."

"That sounds like a good thing to me. Bess could use another woman around."

Dutch didn't respond.

Wade straightened from where he'd been squatted in front of the children's medication. "What's the problem?"

When Dutch's voice came back over the line it was muffled. "They're just sort of a handful."

"All the best women are." Wade grabbed a bottle of Pedialite and added it to the growing pile of items in the red plastic basket.

"That's easy for you to say. You're not here trying to wrangle them." Dutch's keystrokes became louder. "Do you know that woman had our firewall back into place within ten minutes of getting here?"

"That sounds like a good thing too." Wade slowly walked down the aisle of the tiny store, looking for anything he could bring back to Bess. "Isn't that what we hired her to do?"

"But she didn't tell anyone it was back. I could have been back online for three hours. Might have even been able to figure out who the fuck we should be looking at for breaching our system."

"Maybe you should have been nicer to her."

"I was nice to her. She got her panties all in a bunch over what she thought I was thinking." Dutch got louder in his ear.

"*Were* you thinking that?"

It was a second before Dutch responded. "I was just surprised."

Wade laughed. "It sounds like she called you out on your bullshit and you're the one who's

172

pissed off." His eyes caught on a box of chocolates. He snagged them. "Better watch out or you'll fall in love.

Dutch snorted in his ear. "Wouldn't do me any good. She's got *fuck off* written all over her forehead."

"Too bad for you then." Wade glanced to where Brock was just finishing up his own shopping and gave him a nod. "Gotta go. We should be back in an hour." Wade disconnected the phone and pushed it into the pocket of his white tactical pants as he met Brock at the checkout. "Dutch is scared of the new hacker."

Brock shook his head. "She better watch out or he'll fall in love with her."

"Yup." Wade unloaded his basket onto the counter and waited while the cashier scanned and bagged the assortment of baby items and candy. Once he was done paying, he collected his bags and pulled out the keys to the Rover. "I'll go out and get our map pulled up."

Wade started the engine and had the directions to their next stop ready by the time Brock slid into the passenger's seat. "You think we're going to find anything?"

"No." Wade backed out of the lot and pulled onto the road. Snow was stacked a few feet high at each side, which wasn't abnormal for this area, but it was a little early to have that much. Yesterday's heavy snowfall put them well over the average for November. The weather in Alaska wasn't for the faint of heart, and this year was a perfect example.

As the SUV made its way out of Brisbane's limits, more snow started to fall, fast and thick, making the roadway almost impossible to see in a matter of minutes.

Wade stared out the windshield, watching the asphalt disappear, leaving little more than a shadowy drop in the snow to use as a guide.

"They're from here. Have to be."

Brock shoved a Twizzler into his mouth. "Who?"

"The team that breached our system. They were out during the snow yesterday. Anyone who wasn't used to it would have waited." Wade squeezed the wheel as his mind worked through everything that happened. "The team of two might not be from here though, and I'm almost positive they're not working together."

Brock slowly chewed on the candy in his mouth. "You think they even know about each other?"

Wade shook his head. "No, but it might help our cause if they did." He held one hand out, palm up, until Brock passed over a rope of Twizzler. He bit off the end, correcting as the tires of the large vehicle skidded on the slippery surface. "Let's hit this lead. Hopefully they're there and we can set up a meet and greet between our new friends."

Brock smiled wide. "Hell yes."

Thirty minutes later they were on foot, creeping through the snow, circling where a small block house was set at the center of a grove of trees.

"See anything?" Dutch's voice in his ear sounded calmer than it did on the phone earlier.

Hopefully that meant things were going better at the cabin.

"Nothing yet. We're still too far away." Brock's tone was low over the line connecting them.

They'd parked the SUV farther away than normal, wanting to be sure anyone hunkered down in the tiny building never had any clue they'd been visited.

Wade slowed his steps. "I think I hear something." He stopped completely, barely tilting his head toward the mechanical sound. "Generator."

"That explains why we didn't see any smoke." Brock's voice was a little louder. "I think you're right about these guys not being together."

"You don't think the two teams are connected?" Dutch's voice was a little higher pitched, the way it went when he was taking a hunch and already running with it.

"If the twosome is here, they definitely aren't as skilled as the larger team." Wade dropped to his stomach and crawled into the brush surrounding the building they were scoping out. "No one in their fucking right mind would run a generator when they were going around pissing people like us off. They'd want to be sure they could hear us coming."

"I know I would." Brock's voice was low and slow.

"You see someone?" Wade leaned into the scope of his long gun, peering through, trying to get eyes on the house.

"Matter of fact I do." Brock had a smile in his words. "Want me to shoot him?"

"Hell yeah, I do." Wade shifted a little, easing toward a line of sight that looked to be a little clearer. "But I'm thinking they might be more useful alive."

"I hate when you guys do this shit." Dutch was pounding on the keys now. "I can't help you if you only understand each other."

"We need to pit these guys against each other." Wade pushed forward in the pack of snow. "We need to work up some extra prints before we go."

"Look at you. Thinkin' ahead." Brock grunted a little.

"Everything okay?" Dutch's typing stopped.

"Just took a tree branch to the dick." Brock blew out a breath. "I think I'm as close as I can get."

"What do you see?" Dutch went quiet, listening.

Wade waited along with him. The overgrowth on this side of the property was impossible to see through, which meant he was going to have to rely on Brock to get as much intel as possible.

"Truck and trailer are there. So's the sled." He was quiet for a minute before continuing. "One came out to check the generator. Got real jumpy in the cold. Haven't set eyes on the other one."

"Can you get me some shots of the plates on the truck?"

"Sure thing."

The line went quiet again as Wade waited for Brock to take the pictures Dutch wanted.

"Got 'em."

"I think we're done then." Get out and get back before these girls go on a rampage again.

Wade was about to shift from his spot when the sound of footsteps froze him in place. "Don't move, Brock."

"Copy."

Wade tucked his nose and mouth into the knit neckline of the heavy coat he wore, catching the fog of his breath. He waited as the steps came closer. It would only be a matter of time before whoever it was saw his tracks. Even with the still-falling snow, it would be obvious to anyone with any sort of experience that someone had been there very recently.

The steps slowed and Wade weighed his options. The amount of time he had to strike first was limited, but so was his visibility. Taking out someone uninvolved wasn't worth the risk.

But neither was the possibility of getting taken out himself. Leaving Bess on her own. Especially considering her situation seemed to get worse by the minute.

Wade carefully worked his way onto his back and waited.

"There's no one on my side, brother. It's all you." Brock's voice was barely audible in his ear. "I'm looking and I can barely see movement. Looks like there's only one."

Brock hadn't had eyes on the second man in the party of two that paid them a visit two days ago. He would be the most likely to be circling the property, especially if the place didn't have cameras. Knowing he was dealing with someone less than skilled eased his mind a little, but sometimes inexperience made men more dangerous instead of less.

The steps were almost on top of him, closing in on the spot Wade entered the trees, when another sound joined their steady pace.

The tell-tale grind and squeak of tires fighting for traction cut through the icy air, echoing through the trees from the direction of the snow-covered drive that led to the small building.

The steps stopped for a second then picked up speed, racing right past Wade's hidden spot, toward the sound of the poorly-controlled vehicle.

"We got company." Brock was a little louder now. "Looks like a real nice BMW."

"Sedan or SUV?" Dutch was back in his ear, ready to tackle this new information.

"SUV." Brock let out a low whistle. "Mr. Fancypants got real dressed up for his trip to The Last Frontier."

"Tall. Blond. Good-looking?" Dutch tossed out descriptors like he had a mark in mind.

Which meant he did.

And Wade had a bad fucking feeling he knew exactly who Dutch believed it to be.

"You forgot stick up his ass." Brock snorted. "He's barking like hell at our guys."

"How about you two get outta there while everyone's distracted."

"No." Wade shifted back, trying to find a spot where he could get eyes on the piece of shit that hurt Bess.

Who took Parker.

"Don't do this Wade. We need these guys." Brock's words carried a warning tone.

"No one needs that motherfucker." Wade found a tiny gap in the jutting branches and piles of snow and peered through his scope. "The world is definitely better off without that piece of shit. Isn't that our fucking rule?"

"You kill him then we've got no way to flush out the real danger to Bess. These dicks aren't a real threat. They blew their wad already." Brock was breathless in his ear. "Let him live at least a few more days."

"He doesn't deserve it." Wade's finger rested against the trigger as the three men came into view, partially obscured by the thin needles of a fir tree still blocking his sight line. "He deserves to die."

"Didn't say he didn't deserve to die. I said we need him to be alive."

A second later someone latched onto Wade's ankles, dragging him backward through the snow.

"Jesus Christ you're heavy." Brock groaned and huffed as he hefted Wade out of the woods and rolled him to his back. He bent over him. "Stop looking at me like you're going to shoot me."

"I might." Wade glared up at his partner. "I had him."

"No way." Brock held out one hand. "Those trees are thick as hell. You would have missed him and then those dumbasses would have lit up the woods trying to shoot back." He gave up waiting and grabbed Wade's hand, hauling him to his feet. "Come on." He took off toward the back of the house. "We might be able to muddy up the waters just enough to confuse the shit outta them. Not that it looks like it will take much."

Wade twisted his head to one side and then the other, trying to stretch out the tension building between his shoulder blades.

Chris was in his sight. Literally.

"Stop fucking pouting and lay some tracks." Brock pointed to the back end of the property where there would be no chance Wade could see anything happening down at the tiny building. He was half way across his assigned area when gunshots sent him ducking for cover.

"The fuck was that?" Wade squinted through the trees at the tiny bit of light coming off the small house. A second later the brightness amped up twofold.

Headlights.

Brock's steps padded through the soft layer of snow as he moved in beside Wade. "Looks like we might not have them as a distraction after all."

They skirted the tree line, watching as the headlights moved up the slippery slope of the deteriorated drive. The expensive SUV careened to one side, narrowly missing a tree, before it finally made it to the road and took off, tires spinning as they kicked up the new layer of snow.

"I think we need to get the fuck out of here." Brock dropped down as the SUV spun out, grabbing Wade's arm and pulling him farther into the cover of the trees.

At first Wade thought Chris was just struggling with the advanced driving required in Alaska, but the SUV kept coming.

"He's coming back."

"Cover and hold while I get you guys backup." Dutch's voice carried a tightness that was unusual for him.

Chris came to a skidding stop in front of the cabin and jumped out before rushing into the small house. A few minutes later he returned, tucking a stack of papers into the inner pocket of his well-cut jacket as he hurried back to his BMW, where he once again struggled up the drive before fishtailing down the road.

Wade waited until his taillights had been gone a handful of minutes before he started down the small incline toward the house. "You still there, Dutch?"

"Always."

"I'm going in."

"You sure that's a good idea?"

"I think we have to." Wade moved down the hill with Brock trailing at his back. Both men moved in tandem, each anticipating the other as they worked as a single unit, a skill they'd perfected over the years they'd spent together.

"We need cleaners." Brock spun to move back to back with Wade, each man watching the space around them, listening to the silence that was always anything but. "Send them to start at the back and work their way around. We tried to leave a trail to confuse them, but—"

Wade bumped open the door to the house. "Doesn't look like that's an issue anymore." He crept across the filthy floor toward where the first man laid flat on his back, arms at his sides.

With a bullet hole in the center of his forehead.

"Shit." Brock peeked beside him. "That's fucking efficient."

Wade pushed down the unease trying to creep in before it could feed the one thing that would prevent him from keeping Bess and Parker safe.

Fear.

He'd never been scared in his life. Not when guns were pointed in his face.

Not when bullets sailed by his body.

But staring down exactly what Chris Snyder was capable of sent a chill down his spine.

This wasn't something most people could do. Shooting someone sounded simple enough, but when push came to shove, ninety-nine percent of the human race wouldn't be able to pull the trigger.

Chris did it without flinching.

Twice.

Wade moved to where the second man was twisted beside the back door, one hand stretched toward it. He'd been reaching as he went down, shot twice in the back by the man hunting Bess and Parker.

The man who might be much more dangerous than Wade gave him credit for.

"Reed and Abe are raking the tracks. Jamison and Tyson are headed your way to clear the rest. Don't leave a fucking trace." The tight edge of Dutch's voice was still there.

"What's the problem?" Wade backed from where the second man fell, following the same path he used before on his way to the door where Jamison and Tyson would be in a matter of minutes. "What did you find?"

"I think you better get back here as soon as you can." Dutch's tone was getting more tense with each passing second.

"Otherwise you'll go crazy."

CHAPTER 14

"HEY." WADE STOOD in the doorway of the cabin she'd been locked in for four days, eyeing her cautiously.

Smart man.

"Hey." Bess stared him down, arms crossed over her chest. "How were your *errands*?"

Wade shifted on his feet, a plastic bag dangling from one hand. "Fine."

"Oh really?" She stepped forward, closing in on him. "That's an interesting assessment of the scene of a double homicide."

Wade's eyes snapped to where Dutch was brewing another pot of coffee in the kitchen. Dutch shook his head. "Don't look at me. I didn't tell her shit."

"So we're back where we started." Bess slow stepped around the man who just put his life in extreme danger without so much as a heads-up. "Half-truths and omissions."

"Told you she was going to be a handful." Shawn speed walked through the great room and shoved a stack of papers into Wade's free hand. "Here's the court papers on the warrant. I've got Charles working on it. He said he should have something worked out before the end of the day."

"Worked out?" Bess crossed her arms over her chest. "And you didn't think it was relevant to tell me what was going on with my own freaking arrest warrant?"

Shawn backed away, working his way toward the office, his hands lifting just a little.

"Probably afraid you'd cry what with you having a vag and all." Harlow sat on the sofa, Converse sneakers kicked up on the coffee table and computer balanced on her lap. "We are delicate flowers."

Bess pressed one finger between her eyebrows, trying to ease the tension building in her head. "Whatever."

She needed a break from all these people. The never-ending chaos unfolding every time she blinked.

Without another word Bess turned and walked away, escaping to the least-populated place in the house.

The only place where she could be alone.

The large bedroom no longer felt like the oasis it did her first day here. Now it was just another place. One more spot where the fear that permeated her life had been able to eke in and take over.

She paused at the side of the bed, resting one hand on Parker's belly, watching as he took slow, even breaths. There had been so many moments just like this one. Where it felt like the control of her own destiny rested in someone else's hands.

Like she was helpless.

"Bess?"

She hadn't even heard the door open. Not surprising considering what Wade did on a regular basis. "I just want to be alone."

"That's not an option right now." Wade's deep voice was closer.

Bess closed her eyes, digging up as much resistance as she could muster. She wanted to be against him, holding him tight.

But throwing something at his stubborn ass was also an appealing thought. "You said you were going to tell me everything."

"I know." He was right behind her now, his body ghosting against hers. "I should have told you."

"Then why didn't you?"

He let out a long, slow breath. One that was filled with both resignation and regret. "Most people can't handle the truth of what I do, Bess."

"Did you kill those men today?" She'd only been able to pick up bits and pieces of what happened. By the time Harlow hacked into the audio line they were using, most everyone had gone quiet.

"No." Wade's hands came to rest on her hips. "It was someone else."

There was an off tone to his voice. Bess spun to face him, anger flaring hot and fast. "Still? You're still holding back?"

Wade's dark eyes searched hers. "This isn't easy for me, Bess."

"It could be. All you have to do is tell me the truth." She stood straight, head high. "I'm not going to break. I haven't yet."

One big hand came to cradle her face. "I don't want you to ever be scared. Not anymore." He pulled her a little closer. "Telling you something I know will scare you is fucking painful for me, do you understand that?"

It was almost impossible to swallow. Whether it was from Wade's closeness or the potential information he was holding was a toss-up. "Just tell me."

Wade's eyes locked onto hers. "It was Chris."

Her whole body went cold. "How do you know that?"

"Because I saw him." Wade paused, hesitating just a little before twisting the knife slicing through what was left of her shredded world. "Chris is here."

His hold on her tightened as her body started to sway a little, the room getting darker than she remembered.

Somehow the thought of Chris sending someone else to do his dirty work made it less scary. Less personal.

But now. Now he was here to be certain his plans were carried out. Whatever they might be.

"Are you sure it was him?"

"The guy drove a BMW SUV. Black." He stepped closer, his chest pressed tight to hers, the wide expanse of his body feeling like a barrier between her and the reality of how much worse things were getting. "Dutch ran the plates." His lips barely brushed her forehead, resting against her skin. "It was him."

"He's here." She could barely choke the words out. This wasn't supposed to happen. He was supposed to be in Oregon. Was *legally required* to be in Oregon. "They gave him an ankle monitor. He can't just take it off. He'll have to go to jail."

Wade's arms came fully around her, wrapping her in a strong embrace. "I think that might be the least of his worries right now." He was quiet for a minute, just holding her in the dark room while her son slept behind them. Finally he took a breath.

"I should have listened to you."

"About?"

"Dutch thinks everything that's happening is connected."

"So does Harlow." Bess buried her nose in the thermal fabric of Wade's shirt, breathing deep as she tried to sort through the mess of emotions clawing at her from every side. Fear. Anger. Disbelief.

For two years she'd been strong. Been brave. Been unbreakable. And all that time she'd been dealing with Chris on her own. Sure her family had been behind her, but someone having your back isn't the same as someone putting themselves in front of you.

Sacrificing whatever it took to keep you safe.

Like she had now.

So why did she suddenly feel weaker? Shouldn't having Wade there make her feel even more brave?

"I thought Harlow was dealing with the breech?"

Bess smiled a little in spite of everything. "She did that in like an hour."

"An hour?"

"Maybe it took a little longer." Bess glanced at the door leading to the great room. "And she had a little downtime while her program was scanning all the data."

There was a knock at the door. A second later it cracked open and Dutch's head barely edged in. "Wade. We gotta do this now."

Bessie's arms tightened around Wade's waist, the gnaw of fear she'd been fighting for what felt like forever biting with an unusual level of ferocity. "What are you doing now?"

"Not me." He slid one hand into hers. "We." Wade stepped back, pulling her along with him. "We have a briefing to attend."

"Now they want to tell me things?" Bess held firm, keeping her feet planted on the thick rug covering the bedroom floor.

"You aren't our usual client, Sweetheart. Most of them only get what we absolutely have to give them, and nine times out of ten they can't even handle that." He gave her a slow smile. "Not one of them has ever been like you."

"How am I?" She was fishing. Shamelessly. But right now Bess needed the bolster.

"You are fucking terrifying." His thumb and finger caught her chin in a gentle pinch. "You scare the shit out of Dutch and Shawn."

Bess pressed down on the smile his words threatened to create. "I doubt that."

"It's true. It's probably also why they're scared to tell you anything. They're afraid you'll ask questions they haven't thought of."

"Isn't that a good thing?"

"Not if it makes you question their ability to keep you safe. That's the reason we're all here, Sweetheart. Because we're the best, and you make them wonder if it's true." Wade was still smiling, pride written all over his face.

"Why do you look so happy about that?" Bess twisted her lips, fighting her own smile as the fear and worry eased, shoved away by Wade's obvious belief in her.

"Because you're mine." He pulled her close again, stealing back any space Dutch's arrival put between them. His hand braced against her jaw, holding with a careful touch as his mouth caught hers in a breath-stealing kiss that only lifted her spirits higher. When he finally pulled away his voice was a little rough, his breathing a little ragged. "I'm sorry I didn't tell you what was going on today, Bess. I will do my best not to let it happen again."

"I was scared. I heard Dutch talking and could tell something was wrong." The cold hand of fear wormed its way through her chest at the memory. "When I heard someone was shot—" Bessie's voice caught.

She expected Wade's guilt to grow. Anticipated another apology.

Maybe a little groveling.

That wasn't what she got.

"Fuck, Sweetheart." He pulled her body tight against his. "You know how to make a man willing to beg for indecent things, you know that?"

"I've made it pretty clear there would be no begging involved." Bess hooked her hands into the loops of his pants and held him tight to her, hoping to get just a little more friction where she wanted it most. As nice as the things Wade had given her were, they weren't sex.

Penetration. Rhythmic, powerful, fucking.

And the deep fear she felt thinking he was in danger only made her need it more. Need *him* more.

She let go of Wade's pants and ran her hands up his chest, fingers sliding over the solid wall of muscle on their way to fork into the short strands of his dark hair. "I can beg though if that would help." She arched against him, her nipples drawing tight as the fabric between their bodies rubbed against the sensitive tips. "I was so scared you were hurt today, Wade. Worried I would never see you again." She pushed up on her toes, ghosting her lips over his. "I thought you left me again."

An instant later she was on her back, pressed into the mattress by the weight of Wade's body over hers.

The sound of Dutch clearing his throat made them both look to the door.

"Still here."

Wade's forehead dropped to rest against her sternum. "Fuck." One deep breath later he was back off the bed, hefting her after him and pulling her quickly toward the door. He shot Dutch a glare as they passed. "Make this fast."

Never in a million years did she imagine herself trying to get busy in a house full of strangers.

Virtual strangers.

But desperate times and all that.

Wade dragged her through the great room where Harlow was still on the couch, Beats covering her ears, computer on her lap. Bess pulled her hand from Wade's and bent over the back of the sofa, lifting one muff from the other woman's ear. "Meeting time."

Harlow slid the headphones down, letting them rest against the back of her neck. "So?"

"The boys are ready to play nice."

"For the record we were always ready to play nice." Dutch took a small step back when Harlow's blue eyes landed on him. "You were the one looking for a fight."

Harlow snapped her computer closed before kicking her feet off the table and onto the floor. "Is that how you remember it, Pretty Boy?" She pushed up from the couch and sauntered toward where Dutch stood.

His eyes narrowed as she advanced on him. "What the fuck did you just call me?"

"I think you heard me." Harlow wore a smile as she slowed in front of him. One black-polish-tipped finger reached out to trace down the front of Dutch's well-cut button-down shirt. *"Pretty Boy."*

His nostrils barely flared as they stared each other down.

"Get it together, Dutch." Shawn stepped between the two, his gaze trained on Harlow. "If you want to stay on you're going to have to learn to work together, Mowry."

Her eyes moved to Shawn, small smile still in place. "Never said I wanted to stay on." Harlow glanced over one shoulder at Bess. "I'll save you a seat." She strutted her way past Dutch and Shawn and into the large office.

Shawn grabbed Dutch by the shoulder as he started to follow her in. "Sit next to her. Let's see how she handles being in the hot seat."

Dutch gave him a nod, but the thin line of his mouth said he was anything but in agreement with Shawn's plan.

Before Bess could take a step Shawn's attention was on her. "You too." He pointed at her. "You know this prick better than anyone. We need your input."

Bess glanced at the bedroom. "What about Parker?"

Wade backed toward the room. "I got him." His eyes flicked to the open office door and then back to her. "You go in. I'll be there in a few."

Bess squared her shoulders. She was not the kind of woman who crumpled on the floor at the first sign of danger. She'd proved that more than once.

She fought Chris every step of the way, stood up to every threat he tried to make.

Now it was time to figure out how to get ahead of him. To be the one making the threats.

Bess walked through the door to find most of the men she'd met over the past few days seated around the long table. She made her way to where Harlow and Dutch sat at the head of the table, and took the seat just around the corner from the only other woman she'd seen since her arrival in Alaska.

Wade came in just as Shawn was closing the door, a still-sleeping Parker tucked in his arms. He sat at Bessie's other side and leaned in. "He's still warm." He pressed the palm of one hand over her son's forehead. "Are you sure it's his teeth?"

Bess nodded. "He's getting four at once." She stroked the soft skin of Parker's cheek with one finger. "This happened last time he had some coming in."

"I got him some Tylenol at the store." The concern in Wade's eyes as he studied the toddler in his arms went straight to her heart, squeezing it tight.

"Thank you." She glanced up as his gaze shifted to her.

His face was serious. "You don't have to thank me for helping take care of him, Bess. Not ever."

"I think we need to get started." Dutch stood from his seat as Shawn reached back to dim the lights. With the click of a remote, Dutch switched on a projector pointed at a large bare whiteboard at the opposite end of the room that served as a makeshift screen.

With another click a photo filled the board.

Bess couldn't stop the air from rushing out of her body at the sight of Chris. It wasn't clear, but the man in the grainy image was unmistakable. "That's him."

Dutch nodded. "This is our primary target. Name is Christopher Snyder Jr., son of Senator Christopher Snyder Sr." He clicked the small remote again and the screen changed. "This is the vehicle he was driving today. Black BMW SUV, license plate one Hotel Oscar Tango Mike Foxtrot."

Harlow looked her way. "His plate is *one hot motherfucker*?"

Heat crept across her skin. How could she have been so stupid? So blind? "He's a twat."

Harlow lifted her hands. "I'm not judging." She pointed to the screen. "I saw the guy. He's not wrong."

Dutch's eyes widened. "He just killed two men."

Her gaze whipped to where Dutch was still staring her way. "How many men have you killed, Pretty Boy?" She leaned toward him. "And don't tell me none."

"Stop." Shawn slapped one hand onto the table. "We're here for a fucking reason, and it's not to watch you two's fucked-up version of foreplay."

Harlow's mouth dropped open. "I would never fuck him."

Dutch's lips twisted into a smug smile. "You sure wouldn't hate me nearly as much if you did."

"Jesus Christ." Shawn leaned across the table and snatched the remote from Dutch's hand, flicking through a few more shots from the outside of a small building set into the middle of a bunch of trees. Without warning, a close-up of a man filled the large board.

A dead man.

It should have disturbed her more than the sight of her ex, especially considering there was a jagged hole in the center of his forehead.

But that wasn't what Bess was focused on.

She pushed up from her seat, staring at the pale, mottled skin and slightly crooked nose.

"I know him."

CHAPTER 15

"YOU'RE KIDDING." WADE watched Bess as she stared at the photo of one of the men Chris killed. He grabbed the remote from Shawn's hand, flipping to the next photo. "What about him?"

The remaining color drained from her face. "These were the men he killed?"

Wade reached for her, hoping to catch Bess before she went down. She slapped at his hand as he tried to pull her into the chair. "I'm fine."

Her eyes didn't leave the screen. "Were those the same men who were here?"

"Yes." Wade waited as she chewed her lower lip. "Flip back to the other picture."

He did as she directed. "Who are these men, Bess?"

Her head slowly moved from side to side, brows coming together. "It doesn't make any sense." She turned to Harlow. "They were contractors. Heating and air. In Wayfield."

Harlow's fingers flew over the keyboard of her laptop. "You got a name?"

Bess looked back at the dead man populating the large screen. "His name is Rodney Brooks." She tapped one finger on the table in a slow, steady drum. "I think the other guy is Dennis Markum."

"Got 'em." Harlow yanked the cord from Dutch's computer and shoved it into the port on the side of hers, ignoring his protests. A second later her computer screen appeared on the wall, a photo of two men standing side by side filling the space. "Looks like them."

Bess nodded. "That's them."

"How does Chris know them?" Wade shifted in his seat as Parker started to stir, rousing from his nap.

Bess stared at the screen as if she hadn't heard him.

"Sweetheart?"

She blinked, head snapping his way. "What?"

"How did Chris know them?"

She shook her head. "He didn't."

The room was quiet for a minute.

Wade decided not to point out that he obviously did, and opted to get information that might actually be more relevant. "How do *you* know them?"

Bessie's attention moved back to the screen. "They were one of the contractors my family's company used."

The silence in the room continued for what felt like forever. It was the sort of quiet that said more than any collection of words could.

Harlow blew out a loud sigh as she kicked back in her seat. "Well that's bad fucking news."

Bess slowly nodded. "It is, isn't it?"

Parker started to fuss in his arms. "Ma-ma-ma-ma." He leaned toward Bess, tiny fingers grabbing for the woman who stood strong and straight at their side.

When she turned to her son, her face showed no sign of the fear that Wade knew had to be fighting through her. The smile she gave Parker was soft and sincere. "Come here, big boy." She hefted him into her arms and held him close. Somehow her spine became even straighter, her jaw more set. "Anyone got a dry-erase marker?"

Shawn slid one toward her across the table. Bess caught it and immediately went toward the large whiteboard that also served as their digital screen. "Can you turn that off, Harlow?"

"Hell yeah." The screen switched off just as Bess stepped up to it.

"They know you. Could identify you easily." Harlow was up too, moving in beside Bess. "Might even be able to get you to come with them."

Bess snorted. "Fat chance on that one. We had to fire them because they weren't showing up to jobs."

Harlow's head snapped to one side, her blue eyes on Bess. "So they were pissed at you."

The two women stared at each other for a second. Finally Bess nodded. "I didn't technically fire them, but I certainly suggested it." She started writing across the board again. "I also might have accused them of theft."

Parker started to sniffle a little. Bess pressed her hand against his head, marker still tucked between two fingers. She looked back at Wade. "Could you bring me the Tylenol you got?"

"Yup." Wade stood up, pushing back from the table as the men seated around it continued to watch the two women work through all the information they had. Shawn stood with him and followed Wade out through the great room and into the kitchen where the bag from the drug store sat on the counter.

"She's something, isn't she?"

Wade glanced up at Team Rogue's mission coordinator but didn't reply. Shawn was going somewhere with this, and he wasn't sure if it was going to piss him off or make him proud. Maybe both.

"Makes sense why you've been such a dick for the past couple of years." Shawn leaned against the counter as Wade opened the cardboard sleeve and dropped the bottle of red liquid into his hand. The other man watched closely as Wade pulled the plastic collar free and read the back label. Finally he laid out the reason for the one-sided conversation.

"What's going to happen when this is all over?"

It was a question Wade had been avoiding. One he didn't have a complete answer to.

But he had enough. "I go where she goes."

Shawn nodded. "That's what I figured." He crossed his arms over his chest. "What if she stayed here?"

"Why would she do that?" Wade eyed the door to the office where Parker was fussing louder.

"Maybe a job offer?"

That caught his attention. Wade focused on Shawn. "You want to offer Bess a job?"

He shrugged. "I want to keep Harlow, and she and your girl are already thick as thieves. I've got a hunch the two of them together might be the piece we've been missing."

Bess and Parker. With him. In Alaska. "I don't know that she will go for it."

Shawn shrugged. "Might not, but I wanted to run it past you before I offered it to her."

"And if I say no?"

Shawn grinned. "Then you'll have to take that up with your lady." He pushed off the counter. "I'm going to offer it to her either way. She's smart as hell. You can almost watch the gears turn in her head." Shawn nodded toward the open office door. "And Harlow is wicked at what she does, so expect the offer to be lucrative."

"Her family's rich. Lucrative won't mean shit to her." Bess wouldn't be swayed by financial gain. She wasn't that kind of woman.

Shawn's gaze stayed on him. "I'm not betting that will be the draw for her." He pointed to the medicine in Wade's grip. "Better take care of your son."

Wade stared at Shawn as he made his way back through the great room.

Thinking he might be a reason for Bess to do anything was more than he could hope for. She had a whole life. A family. Expecting her to leave all that behind for him was asinine.

But he would leave it all behind for her. For them.

Because they were his life now. All that would ever matter. He'd missed out on so much. Good and bad. Parker's first words, first steps.

The opportunity to end this bullshit with Chris before it could grow legs.

Before Bess got hurt.

Now it was time to prove he could make up for all of it and take the one thing he never expected to want.

A family.

Wade was just walking into the room when his cell started to ring. Bessie's eyes met his, one hand frozen mid letter against the board covered in her careful, perfectly straight writing.

He held her gaze, answering the call and putting the phone to his ear.

"This is Michelle with the Alaskan Paternity Lab. I'm looking for Wade Denison."

"This is."

"Hello, Mr. Denison. You should have been given a password. I need that before I can give you the results of the test submitted under your name."

"Lilac shanty." It was a ridiculous code, but one he would never forget as long as he lived.

"Thank you." Michelle went quiet for a second. "Bear with me while I pull up the results."

The room was silent. No one even seemed to be breathing.

And Bessie's hazel eyes never left his. Never wavered as they waited.

"Okay. I have a paternity test that shows the probability of parentage of the samples for Wade Denison and Parker Hines is 99.9%."

Wade didn't move. He thought hearing the truth he knew from the beginning would change something, impact him in some way.

It didn't. Parker was always going to be his, no matter what, because Bess was his. "Thank you."

He disconnected the call and stepped away from the door. "Get out." His eyes finally left Bessie's to scan the shocked faces around him. He pointed at the open doorway. "Everyone. Out."

Brock was the first to stand up. "Come on. He's going to be an ass if we don't move fast enough." He held back as the rest of the group filed out in silence. As he was walking past Wade he grabbed him in a hug, slapping his back as he whispered in his ear. "Congratulations, man." The door shut quietly behind him.

"Already?" Bess was a little pale.

Wade nodded.

"What did they say?" The question was barely a whisper through Bessie's lips.

Wade walked along the side of the long table toward where Bess and Parker were, cranking open the child-proof lid on the medicine bottle as he went. "How much does he weigh?"

Bess blinked at him. "What?"

"How much does Parker weigh?" He lifted the medication. "The label says the dosage depends on how much he weighs."

"Are you kidding?" Bess glared at him. "What did the test show?" She pulled Parker a little closer. "Is he yours?"

Wade stopped at her side, setting the Tylenol and its measuring syringe on the table in front of them before pressing one hand to Bessie's back and one to Parker's. "Sweetheart, that was never in question." He slid one hand up to brush against Parker's dark hair before stepping back to lift the dispensing syringe so he could read the lines. "How much does he need?"

"3.75 milliliters." She waited as he pulled the amount into the plastic syringe.

Wade gently put the tip of the dispenser between Parker's lips and pushed the plunger slowly. Parker didn't flinch, didn't fuss, just sucked the medicine down without complaint. "Good boy."

"Please tell me." The waver in her voice hurt his pride, made him wonder if she knew the truth.

That he didn't care. Never cared.

He never had a father. Never expected to want to be one.

But when the opportunity arose, Wade never batted an eye.

Parker was his. Genetic connection or not.

Wade took a deep breath, setting the empty syringe on the table before finding Bessie's gaze. The fear there broke his heart, stabbed guilt deep into his gut.

And it was his fault. He left her, plain and simple. Thinking a few days of showing her the truth of what happened would change anything was selfish as hell. "Bess," he pulled her and Parker close, resting his head on hers, "he's mine in every way."

The tears weren't completely unexpected. It's why he cleared the room. Letting Bess react to this without an audience was the most important thing.

She needed as much privacy as he could give her right now.

He held her close, cradling both her and Parker against him as she sniffled into his shirt.

After less than a minute she sucked in a deep breath and straightened, head tipping back, chin lifting in the air. "We need to file with the courts. Prove Chris has no claim to him."

"That might not help our cause, Sweetheart." Wade fought the need to pull them close again. "I'm not sure that man is playing with a full deck right now."

Bessie's lips barely lifted. "That's what I'm counting on." She turned to the board, eyes scanning the information neatly laid out. "I think something else is going on but I'm not sure what." She pointed to where her name was at the center of the board. "This might not be only about me, but I'm the common denominator for everything so far." Her eyes turned to him. "And it's time to force him to make a mistake."

Wade was already shaking his head. "I don't know what you're thinking, but it's not happening."

"It's the only way." Bess smoothed Parker's dark hair back. "It's either me or Parker and I think we would both prefer it's me in the line of fire."

"It's not happening." A level of panic he'd never experienced bubbled through him at the thought of either of them being used as bait. "No fucking way."

He knew what it was like to grow up without a parent. Knew how that shaped a person. Dictated the way they lived their whole life. The choices they made.

Bess held firm, chin tipped back, shoulders straight. "I will do anything to protect him, Wade. I don't care what it is."

"There has to be another way." Wade shook his head. "I'm not letting you—"

"Wrong answer." Bess moved past him to the door. She yanked it open. "Everyone come back in. We've got shit to do."

Wade moved in behind her, slamming the door shut with one hand and catching her with the other. "Just because it's what you've always done doesn't mean it's the only fucking way, Sweetheart." He crowded her. "You've been on your own until now, I get that." He shook his head at her. "But things have changed. You aren't the only thing standing between Chris and Parker anymore." Wade pressed her against the door. "He's got a lot of men way fucking scarier than he could ever hope to be that will put their life on the line to keep him from so much as setting eyes on you or our son."

Our son. He didn't even have time to enjoy the sound of the words, because Bess needed to realize there was never just one way to handle what needed to be handled. "And he will have to go through each one of them, understand?"

She blinked up at him. "But it's the easiest way."

"Doesn't matter." Wade gripped her chin, holding her in place so he could do the one thing that would ease the fear gripping him. Bess barely gasped in surprise when his mouth covered hers in a kiss that was a little rougher than Wade wished it was. But that was how he felt right now. A little rough. A little desperate.

He needed her to see it. Know that the thought of her getting hurt made him out of his mind in a way he'd never experienced before.

When he could finally make himself pull away, Parker was watching them with wide eyes.

Bess frowned. "I think he's scarred."

"Good." Wade caught her lips in another kiss, this one a little softer, a little sweeter. "He needs to know his daddy doesn't want to live without his momma." Wade leaned into her ear. "And I'm not going to even try, Sweetheart, so you better buckle up."

Bess sucked in a breath as he caught the lobe of her ear between his teeth and gently raked across the soft bit of flesh. "I hope you enjoyed your time away from me because I'm not sure you're going to get another day without having to look at my face." He pressed his body into hers, careful not to catch Parker between them. "Tonight he's sleeping in his own bed, Bess." Wade leaned back to look in her eyes.

He'd held back. Tried to give her time to adjust to all that was happening.

He wasn't going to hold back anymore. It was time to lay all his cards on the table.

"Because you're all mine."

CHAPTER 16

SHE WAS A failure as a functioning human.

All it took was Wade's proclamation that Parker would be spending the night in his own bed and her brain was gone. Dissolved into nothing but images of his big body over hers. Hot and firm.

Thrusting.

Bess covered her face with her hands.

Harlow reached out to rub her back, leaning into her ear. "It's going to be okay."

Thank God her new friend mistook her sexual frustration for fear. Otherwise she would no doubt question Bessie's sanity.

What kind of woman sat thinking about the sorts of things she was in a situation like this?

Harlow patted her back, eyes filled with sympathy. "You'll be able to bone him soon."

Bess stared at her for a heartbeat before busting out laughing. Harlow joined her a second later, wrapping one arm around Bessie's shoulders.

"I am so freaking glad you're here." Harlow wiped at her eyes. "Otherwise I would have rolled one of them up in a carpet by now."

That only made Bess laugh harder, imagining tiny Harlow trying to drag one of the giant men out of the house. "They're mercenaries."

"I know." Harlow was still laughing. "What the fuck are we doing here? We're locked in a cabin with ten dudes who kill people for a living."

"I don't know." Bess tried to take a slow breath, hoping to calm the cackle of almost-crazed laughter rushing out of her. "At least they're paying you."

"That's true." Harlow eyed where Wade stood beside Shawn, Parker held close to his chest. "But I'm thinking your compensation might be better than mine." She leaned in. "How many people has Wade killed?"

Bess no longer had to fight the borderline insane giggles from seconds ago. The idea of Wade killing someone was like a bucket of water.

Not because it bothered her that he had ended lives.

More because it bothered her that it didn't.

What did that make her?

It made her the kind of woman who thought about fucking at inappropriate times.

Laughed when there was someone trying to kill her.

And didn't care that the man she was falling for was a murderer.

She actually might like him more for it. To her, knowing Wade killed men like Chris was like knowing he rescued kittens.

And that was screwed up.

That's what the past two years had done to her. It made her harder. More cynical. She was no longer the same woman from before. The kind of woman who thought love was sweet and neat and easy. That life was fair, and most people were good.

The naiveté she took for granted was ripped away. Shredded by the sort of evil that could hide right under your nose.

Her nose.

And she hadn't even seen it coming.

Bess shook her head. "I don't know how many people he's killed."

Harlow's lip curled in disappointment. She glanced around the room where the men were working their way through all the scribbles the two women worked out on the board. "What about Dutch? You think he's killed anyone?"

Bess shrugged. "Probably."

Harlow's eyes moved up and down Dutch's tall, lean body, her head bobbing in a slow nod. "Probably." She pursed her lips. "Am I a bad person if that makes me a little hot?"

"God, I hope not." Bess almost jumped when Wade's black eyes moved her way, his gaze settling easily onto hers.

"He's good in bed, isn't he?"

"Yup." Bess couldn't make herself look away until Shawn stepped in, dragging Wade's attention from her. She blinked a few times, trying to right her inverted brain.

Harlow bumped her shoulder to Bessie's. "Lucky girl. I could use a good sexing, myself." She stood from her chair, stretching both arms high over her head. "Enjoy it for me too, 'cause I don't see any dick in my future." She yawned loudly before leaning onto the table. "You boys done with me? I'm fucking tired."

Shawn turned from where he was still discussing something that looked a little tense with Wade. "We get up at five, Mowry. Don't be late."

Harlow lifted one dark brow. "Or what? You'll come drag me from my bed?"

Shawn shook his head. "That's your boss's job. And I'm pretty sure he'd be more than happy to help you out of bed." He tipped back a cup of coffee, hiding a smile as Harlow's eyes flew wide and her cheeks flushed.

"What's that supposed to mean?" Harlow was trying, but she definitely didn't hate the idea of Dutch dragging her across a mattress as much as she wanted everyone to think she did.

"Means he needs your help, and will do whatever it takes to get it." Shawn gave her a smile. "Goodnight, Harlow."

All Harlow gave him back was a glare that would wilt most men.

None of those men seemed to be in this house, which only appeared to irritate Harlow more. One middle finger shot their direction as she stormed from the office, blowing Bess a kiss over her shoulder.

214

Bess blinked hard, trying to ease the burning in her own tired eyes. It was late.

Probably. It was impossible to tell what time it was here. She quietly stood up, planning to sneak away and take a long bath.

"Bess."

Wade's voice snaked down her spine, stopping her in the doorway. She tipped her head to look at him over one shoulder.

"Give me thirty minutes and I'll be in."

She nodded, trying not to choke on the glob of anticipation clogging her throat. "You want me to take Parker with me?"

Parker's head was resting on Wade's shoulder and one chubby-fingered hand patted his bicep. Wade glanced down at their son. "I'll keep him. He'll be asleep in a few minutes anyway."

She nodded. "Okay."

The sight of her son tucked safely in his father's arms was one that would stick with her forever. Because it was something that, until a few days ago, she never thought would be possible.

And the realness of it was almost unbearable.

Parker would never be safer than he was with Wade. Wade would kill to protect him. No questions asked.

Since he was born, Bess struggled to let Parker out of her sight, thinking no one would ever love him like she did.

That no one else would ever be willing to die for him.

She was wrong.

Ten minutes later Bess was dipping her toes into a hot bath, hoping the steam and scalding water would ease the constant tension winding the muscles of her neck and shoulders together. She sank in up to her chin and closed her eyes, relaxing back against the inclined edge of the tub.

A second later she started awake.

"Shhh." Wade was on his knees beside the tub, a giant fluffy towel held between his outstretched hands.

She stared at him for a second before realizing her naked body was bared under the harsh bathroom light, with nothing but lukewarm bathwater between her and Wade's dark gaze.

Which he wasn't even pretending to keep off her.

"Stop looking." Bess started to cover herself, but honestly at this point there were so many places that needed to be hidden she didn't have enough hands to get the job done.

She always thought the primary problem after pregnancy was the weight gain, and figured as long as you could lose it everything would be fine.

One more way she had been so naive it was laughable.

Wade's eyes slowly moved up her form as her hands warred over the parts of her body particularly ravaged by Parker's incubation. Finally his gaze came to rest on her face. "Why are you hiding from me?"

"Because it's all—" Bess looked down at her soft tummy and stretch-mark-covered boobs, "changed."

216

"Thank God it did or we wouldn't be here, would we?" Wade leaned closer, stretched the towel wider. "You would still be in Oregon, and I would still be so fucking miserable I couldn't see straight."

Bess swallowed hard. The thought of a man wanting you for two years after just one night together was flattering, but it also brought a huge amount of pressure to be worth the wait. Worth the misery he claimed.

"I'm different now, Wade." He needed to know she wasn't that same woman from two years ago. The woman who thought she understood people and why they did the things they did. "I'm not the woman you remember."

It was a hard truth to face, because honestly she'd spent the past two years telling herself that everything could be different if only the man she spent one, glorious night with would come back.

But that might not be true.

So far it hadn't been.

Chris was still breathing down her neck. Trying to hurt her in retaliation for some screwed-up belief he had that she cheated on him and ruined everything. And now he was killing people who got in his way.

She was away from the only support she'd had. Her family. Her best friend. Both were probably beside themselves with worry.

And she hadn't had a freaking minute to even think about all of it because she was locked in a cabin packed with virtual strangers.

So actually things had gotten worse.

Most things.

Wade smiled down at her. "I would say I'm probably not the same either, but that's something I consider a good thing." He rocked back onto his heels, holding the towel up. "Come out, Bess."

He wanted her to stand in front of him, naked and wet.

She reached for the towel. He pulled it out of reach, shaking his head. "You are more perfect to me today than you were two years ago." He held the towel up again. "Come on."

The water was getting uncomfortably cool. Bess shivered against the chill easing into her skin.

Wade groaned, his eyes dragging down to the puckered tips of her breasts. "Jesus, Sweetheart. If you're not getting out, I'm getting in."

"The water's cold."

His eyes didn't move. "I see that."

As much as she didn't want to display the extent of the changes her body underwent since he last really saw it, staying in the chilly water was becoming much less appealing of an option. "Close your eyes."

Wade shook his head. "Not a chance that's going to happen." He shook the towel a little. "Come on. Don't be scared."

Her eyes snapped to his. "I'm not scared."

"I didn't expect you would be." Wade's eyes held a sparkle she hadn't seen since coming here.

"Are you teasing me?"

"Maybe." He grinned. "I might also be pushing your buttons to get what I want."

Bess sank down a little in the water. "What is it you want?"

Wade leaned closer, his eyes finding every inch of what she hoped to hide. "You."

"I'm not—"

"Not what you were. I heard." Wade reached into the water, his hands sliding under her body and locking together before he hefted her up and out of the bath. "I also disagree."

Water soaked Wade's shirt and pooled around his feet as he tossed her naked, drenched body against his shoulder. "But you can tell me all about it later."

She hadn't wanted him to see her completely naked in the bright light of the bathroom. It seemed like a reasonable request.

And in hindsight it might have been the lesser of two evils, because now her bare ass was right next to his face. It didn't get any easier to see.

"Please put me down." The calm in her voice was surprising, especially considering right now she was bouncing between full-on panic and complete embarrassment.

"I will, Sweetheart. When I'm good and ready." Wade snagged a couple more towels as they left the bathroom. "I like that you don't do things the easy way." He tossed one towel across the bed and leaned down, carefully rolling her off his shoulder and onto the soft terry cloth. "Makes things way more fun." He shook out the other towel and used it to dry her body, starting at her toes. He worked his way up her legs, large hands gently kneading the muscles of her thighs as he went. "I don't know what I would have done if you hadn't come back to me, Bess." His dark eyes found hers in the dim light of the bedroom. He was quiet for a minute. When he spoke again his voice was soft.

"My dad died when I was too young to remember."

She watched as he moved over her stomach, spending more time than necessary on the lined skin there.

"My mom raised me on her own. I saw how she struggled every fucking day." His jaw clenched tight as his fingers brushed the spot where she grew their son. "I'm sorry I made you do the same thing."

Bess shook her head. "Why do you keep apologizing? Do you think I would ever take that night back?"

His gaze was steady and filled with something she couldn't identify. "I know you would never take Parker back."

Parker.

She would never take Parker back.

"Wade." Bess had been fighting herself since he showed up. Fighting what she knew was real because it didn't seem there could be any way it was.

She'd doubted him. Doubted he wanted her.

Tried to pretend it would be okay if he didn't.

But it wouldn't be okay.

"It's not just Parker I would never take back."

He watched her for what felt like forever.

And then his body was on hers in an instant, hard and hot and...

Wet.

Bess grabbed at the hem of his shirt, trying to fight the water-logged fabric up his chest. "Take this off."

"Yes, ma'am." His weight left her for just a second as Wade peeled the thermal shirt down his arms and tossed it to the floor. When he came back his hot skin pressed into hers, the barely-rough bit of dark hair across his pecs brushing her nipples with the most delicious scrape of friction.

Bess yanked at the fly of his pants, desperate for more of him against her. "These too."

"Demanding." Wade pushed up and worked the button loose. "That's the same as I remember it." He eased down the zipper and stood, fighting down the wet denim. "I like that about you too." Before he tossed them beside his shirt, Wade retrieved a condom from one pocket.

"Only one?"

His brows lifted. "We've got a sleeping baby to juggle, Sweetheart. I was trying to be considerate."

"You just set a precedent I was sort of expecting you to uphold." The night they met he'd accomplished more in a few hours than most men could in a week.

Including knocking her up accidentally, thanks to a less than functional condom.

Wade crawled onto the bed over her. "I'm also checking to be sure nothing is defective this time." His lips found one of her breasts and pulled it deep into his mouth, the tug shooting straight to her core like a lightning bolt of heat. He released it too quickly. "Not that I'm uninterested in giving Parker a little brother."

Bess blinked up at him, struggling to wrap her mind around what he said. "You've got to be kidding."

Wade's head slowly moved side to side. "I went my whole like never wanting this to happen, Bess. Always thinking I wasn't the kind of man who should be a father to anyone."

Her disbelief only grew at the comment. "What?" In the few days he'd been with Parker nothing was more clear than the fact that this man was one-hundred percent cut out to be a dad. He'd taken to caring for Parker like second nature, never missing a beat. "That's the dumbest thing I've ever heard."

"You still don't bullshit. I loved that too." Wade's lips moved to the skin of her neck. "In one night I knew you were exactly what I would have wanted if things had been different, Bess." His words were a whisper against her flesh. "And you made things different. You and Parker decided what I never would."

"We didn't decide anything." Her brain struggled to keep up with the string of words still falling from his lips.

"You did." His hands sank into her hair, cradling her head between his wide palms as he leaned up to look into her eyes. "You decided I should be happy."

Her eyes suddenly felt very wet. "You should be happy."

Wade's smile was barely there, a teasing curve on the line of his full lips. "I am happy." His mouth brushed hers, not leaving even when he started to speak again. "Because of you."

Two years she imagined what would happen if she found him. Thought of every possible way it could go.

Never was it anything like what actually happened. Even her wildest fantasies couldn't touch this perfect moment. Bess pulled him down with a hand at the back of his neck, meeting his mouth with hers as she wrapped her legs around his waist, trying to get closer to the man who might have lied about his name the first night they met, but always showed her who he really was.

"I need you. Right now."

"But—"

She sealed her lips against his, cutting off whatever stupid argument Wade would have for not doing what she wanted. Maybe he was scared. Maybe he was hoping to wait until things were perfect.

Perfect was an illusion created by people with unrealistic expectations, and the past two years had certainly cured her of unrealistic expectations.

Wade tried to pull away again. "Bess—"

"Nope." She pushed one heel into the mattress and shoved hard. The surprise attack worked in her favor, and Wade ended up rolling with her, landing on his back, her knees on each side of his hips. The condom sat at his side and she snagged it, ripping the foil open with her teeth, damp hair falling in her face from the roll across the mattress.

She felt a little wild.

And a lot powerful.

This giant man was beneath her. At her mercy. Cock thick and ready. Eyes dark and filled with need that spoke of more than a physical desire.

Bess sheathed his straining length, and before he could protest, pushed up to her knees and sank down over him, head falling back as he filled her.

His hands gripped her hips, fingers pressing into the soft flesh that had rounded out since their first meeting. "You are fucking magnificent." Wade's eyes roamed her face, her body, his hands following along as they moved over every bit of her as she pushed up and down, riding him with a mindless desire to chase the sort of feelings only he'd ever been able to rouse.

"You feel so good." She pressed her hands into his chest, head falling forward as she found her pace. Bess rocked against him as her body shook, struggling to move as unbearably intense pleasure fought its way through her.

"That's a girl." Wade's grip on her hips tightened and he lifted to meet her. "Take what you want."

His deep voice pushed her higher. The words of encouragement and praise getting more broken. More rough.

"You're so fucking perfect for me, Bess. I knew it the minute I saw you. Knew you would ruin me." The thrusting of his hips carried more force and less control. "And you did. You fucking ruined me."

The tips of her fingers bit into the skin of his pecs as she fought to keep her balance.

"There would never be anyone else like you. I knew it. I knew what we could have had if I wasn't what I am." His hands slid from her hips to her breasts, each one finding an already tight nipple and rolling it between his fingers. "I couldn't bring this life to you, Bess."

She squeezed her eyes shut as the truth settled around them.

Wade would never have brought the danger of his life to her.

She straightened, making herself find his eyes. "I'm here anyway."

He pulled her body down, holding her close. "I swear I'll keep you safe, Bess. No one will hurt you. Not ever." His hips pistoned up, slapping against her as he held her tight against his chest, fucking her from his place beneath her. "I will kill anyone who even fucking tries. No one will take you from me. Not now."

She would have told him the same thing except her throat wouldn't work, her lips couldn't form words. All her body could do was ride the wave of pleasure that chose that exact moment to crest and crash, taking her under with a force that stole her breath.

"That's it, Sweetheart. Come for me." His voice was barely a growl in her ear as he filled her over and over, stretching her climax out until there was no sound. No light. Nothing but the way he made her feel.

With a low groan and his hands wrapped tight in her hair, Wade shoved deep into her, his powerful body jerking in time with the twitching of his cock as he spilled into the condom between them.

Bess went limp. Sagging against him, her body completely spent from something that was so much more than fucking.

Wade's arms held her close, wrapped around her back as he buried his face in her neck, the rhythmic sound of his breathing lulling her into a state of relaxation that could only be felt when a person was completely satisfied.

And when they felt completely safe.

For the first time in a very long time, she was both of those things.

CHAPTER 17

BESS BARELY SHIFTED, curling a little tighter against him.

He'd been avoiding getting out of bed for almost an hour, lying awake with Parker asleep on his chest and Bess sleeping at his side.

But it was time for Parker's medicine, and it only took one time missing it for Wade to realize how quickly his son's fever would spike without it. Apparently cutting teeth was no fucking joke.

Wade carefully eased from under the covers, holding Parker gently as he scooted away from the woman who unknowingly gave him everything he'd been too scared to want.

Parker stirred, whimpering softly.

"Shhh. I know, Buddy." Wade padded barefoot across the bedroom rug, silently opening the door before slipping out into the great room where most of the team was already milling around.

Dutch was at the counter of the open kitchen, scooping coffee into the filter of the 12-cup maker Harlow was filling with water.

"You guys seem to be working together a little better this morning." Wade adjusted Parker so he had a free hand for medication administering.

Harlow's curly hair was wild and unruly, and a shadow of make-up smudged the space just below her eyes. "It's for the greater good." She already had a cup in her hand, one finger tapping the black ceramic side as she watched the coffee drip into the decanter.

"Here it's always for the greater good." Shawn was already dressed, outfitted in his normal khaki pants and button-down shirt. He was as capable as the rest of Team Rogue, and had stepped in on more than one occasion when they needed another set of hands on a job, but Shawn was the only one of them who also possessed the skills needed to juggle the accepting and scheduling of new clients. "Remember that."

"Is it?" Wade sucked the required amount of sticky red liquid into the plastic syringe. "We aren't always on the side of good, Shawn."

The line they walked could go either way depending on the client. Sometimes they worked for good, like Bessie's case. Other times...

There was no good side. Only bad and worse.

"It is now." Shawn pulled a bowl of fruit salad from the fridge and set it on the counter before popping off the lid. "For a long time we took anything and everything that came our way to prove we could." Shawn popped a chunk of melon into his mouth and continued talking as he chewed. "And I don't know about you guys, but I got nothing to prove anymore."

"Maybe that you have some manners." Harlow elbowed him out of her way. "Chew with your mouth shut, caveman."

Shawn grinned at the back of her head as she forked some fruit into a bowl. "I am so damn glad we found you, Harlow."

The hacker who saved their asses continued scooping fruit into her bowl. "I bet."

"I'm serious. Not many people can hold their own with us, and you fit in perfectly." Shawn waited for her to face him before continuing. "Come work for us."

Harlow pulled a grape off her fork with the tips of her teeth, staring at Shawn as she chewed and swallowed. "I'll think about it."

Shawn smiled. "I appreciate it."

"Whatever." Harlow turned away from him, her eyes landing on Parker. She tipped her head to one side so it was even with how Parker's rested against Wade's chest. "You don't look like you feel good."

"He's teething." Wade's heart broke a little when his son's lower lip pushed out. "Bess says this is how it always goes." He carefully wedged the end of the syringe between Parker's pouting lips and slowly pushed the plunger, watching to be sure the toddler didn't spit it back out at him. It happened in the middle of the night, and ended with both of them needing fresh clothes and a wipe down before going back to bed.

LOSS RECOVERY

Parker took the whole dose like a champ before resting his head back on Wade's chest.

"That's some rough teething." Harlow placed one hand on Parker's back. "His little eyes are glassy." Her brow pinched. "I'm so sorry you feel so bad, sweet boy."

"Coffee's done." Dutch stepped in beside Harlow with the full pot of coffee, waiting while Harlow finished cooing at Parker before pouring the first of the steaming-hot liquid into her cup.

A sacrifice that wasn't lost on Wade. Maybe it was a peace offering. Harlow would make Dutch's life a hell of a lot easier if she stayed on at Alaskan Security.

But the first cup of coffee on an early morning was a hell of a sacrifice, especially for Dutch, considering half his blood was probably made of the stuff.

"Charles is coming here this morning to go over what he came up with for you and Bess. Give you two a few options on how you could proceed with things." Shawn held out his own cup as soon as Dutch was finished pouring Harlow's.

"Fuck you." Dutch poured the next bit into his own mug before passing the pot to a grinning Shawn.

Shawn filled his cup then passed it down the line. "I think we need to have a meeting as a team when this is all over. Decide exactly where we want to go from here." His eyes lifted to Wade over the rim of his cup. "I think you've given the guys a lot to consider."

"How's that?" Wade rested back against the counter, cradling his son.

Shawn's gaze fell to Parker. "I think you showed them we might all be reaching the point where we want a little more from life."

Harlow suddenly straightened, smiling brightly. "Good morning." She took her untouched cup of coffee and rushed around the island separating the open kitchen and great room. "Here. You look like you could use this." She shoved the mug into Bessie's hands.

"Thanks." Bess sipped at it while Harlow smoothed down the strands of her blonde hair.

"Looks like you slept good."

"I did." Bess wiped at the corner of one eye. "I haven't slept through the night in freaking forever and it was fantastic."

"Kids'll do that to you." Harlow finished rectifying Bessie's wayward locks and stepped back. "I think yours is feeling a little crappy this morning."

Bess moved past Harlow, heading straight for where Wade and Parker were propped against the kitchen counter. "Is he doing any better?"

"I just gave him his medicine." Wade watched as she stroked their son's head. "He doesn't seem to be any worse, but he's definitely not any better either."

Bess frowned. "Usually the fever doesn't hit him quite this hard." Her palm pressed against Parker's forehead. "Hopefully it's because he's getting a few at once."

"Could he be sick?" It was a concern Wade had been reluctant to voice, as if not putting it out there could prevent it from being the truth.

Bessie's hazel eyes lifted to meet his. "I hope not."

"If he is, we will deal with it." Wade reached for her with his free arm and pulled her body close, holding her tight as he pressed a kiss to her forehead. "We will do whatever it takes to make sure he's okay."

Bess nodded, staying quiet for a second before straightening a little as she looked at the faces in the room. "Don't you guys have other jobs?"

Shawn shrugged. "I thought it was important that we all be here." His eyes barely flicked to Wade and Parker before moving back to Bess. "I had one other job on the books, but moved it to one of our other teams."

Bessie's head barely tipped to one side. "Why?"

"Lots of reasons." Shawn swallowed down the last of his coffee.

"What else is happening that I don't know about?" Bess pushed against Wade, her eyes snapping to his. Accusation sat in their almost-green depths.

"You know everything Wade knows, Bess." Shawn studied her for a minute. "You're perceptive as hell, you know that?"

Bessie's eyes narrowed on him, sitting squarely on his face and staying there. "Doesn't take a lot to see you're not telling me something."

Wade glanced from Bess to Shawn. He hadn't realized Shawn was keeping something. Didn't have a clue the other man was withholding information. Not until Bess suggested it.

Now it was written all over his face.

"What's going on, Shawn?" Wade pulled Bess closer, held Parker tighter.

Shawn shook his head. "Relax. It's got nothing to do with your family."

The relief Wade should have felt was washed away by a more powerful emotion.

Peace.

Your family.

He'd never had a family. He had his mother. That was it. He'd grown up as the man of the house in a world that no child should have to experience. But it was the best his mother could give him.

And he'd done everything it took to get them both out of there. And he had.

But it all came at a cost. One he thought he was happy to pay.

Until he met Bess.

"After Charles leaves I'm calling everyone in for a meeting so we can go over some things." Shawn topped off his coffee. "I think the direction of the team is beginning to shift and I want us all to be on the same page." Shawn backed toward the office. "Charles should be here in a few so you might want to be ready."

"Understood." Wade watched him go before leaning into Bessie's ear. "I can take care of Parker while you get dressed."

She pulled her eyes from where they still followed Shawn. "What do you think he's keeping from everyone?"

"I'm sure it's not a big deal." He was not sure of that at all, but the last thing Bess needed was more to worry about. He'd lied to his mother a thousand times as a kid, always to protect her from the truth. Whether it was not having enough money to buy lunch, or how the electric bill was paid once he was old enough to earn money himself, Wade always told his mother only what he had to.

But his mother was different from Bess. While Bess was resilient and unbreakable, his mother was fragile. Delicate in spite of the strength she showed the outside world.

And treating Bess like his mother wasn't fair.

Wade leaned closer. "I *hope* it's not a big deal."

Her eyes found his. "But?"

"But I've never known Shawn to keep something from us." Wade held his breath, watching to see how the truth settled with Bess.

"He said it wasn't about me. Would he lie?" She was working her way through it, trying to decide how she felt about the situation. He loved that about her. Bess didn't make snap judgments or jump to immediate conclusions. She was careful, breaking down every aspect of a problem and analyzing it, before coming to her own conclusion.

Wade shook his head. "He wouldn't lie."

"So if it's not about me, then it must be about you." Her lips pressed together, rubbing slowly from side to side. "I don't know that I like that any better."

Wade smiled in spite of the fact that she was most likely right. "Sweetheart, I just found you. It will take an act of God to get me away from you and Parker."

He thought that might make her smile. Might ease the worry in her gaze. Instead her eyes sharpened. Nostrils flared. "I tried to kill him once. I won't mess up if I get a second shot at that bastard."

The comment sat wrong. "What do you mean, you tried to kill him once?"

Bess held up her arm, the light catching on the thin, shiny lines across the skin of her forearm. "It's sort of how I got this."

"I thought he attacked you?" He read the charges against Chris. It clearly stated assault in addition to kidnapping. Initially Wade thought both of those involved Bess.

"It was more mutual than the charges make it sound."

"So he kidnapped Parker. You jumped on his car. Then," Wade eyed the scars on her arm, doing his best not to let the rage biting at him creep into his voice, "you tried to stab him."

Bess let out a loud sigh. "It was a stupid idea in hindsight, but it was all I had at the time." She dropped her arms, the fingers of her right hand skimming over the scars she earned protecting her son from a man who was capable of more than she could have ever imagined at the time. "I went a little crazy I guess." She continued to absentmindedly stroke the slices. "I was so careful to avoid the glass too."

Wade tried to hide his confusion. "The glass?"

Bess nodded. "I threw a rock through the window on the door to his house so I could reach in to unlock it."

"You followed him to his house and then threw a rock through his window. Then went inside and tried to stab him." Wade was doing his best to follow along, but the story was turning out to be more involved than he expected.

"Well, I followed him to his house and made sure he couldn't use his car to get away." Her lips twisted into a little smile. "That's why he has that brand new SUV. Then I threw the rock and successfully stabbed him."

Wade stared at her.

Bess stared back. "What?"

"He's hot and wants to bone again." Harlow edged in beside them on her way back to the coffee pot. "But he's sad you don't have time because you have to get ready to see the lawyer guy who's coming over."

Harlow was off-base as hell, but Wade wasn't pointing that out in front of her. He wanted Harlow on his side, especially considering how much Bess seemed to like her. "She's right. We need to get ready."

Harlow's eyes widened as Shawn stepped into the hall, looking directly at her. "Jesus. I'm coming back." She rolled her eyes. "I don't know how you put up with him." She tipped back her coffee as she made her way to the office where Shawn and Dutch were waiting on her.

Shawn closed the door behind her.

Interesting.

Wade pulled Bess toward the front bedroom. "And she's wrong by the way. Knowing you put yourself in that kind of position does not make me hot." The thought of her doing it made him fucking insane actually.

And the problem was there wasn't a doubt in his mind Bess would do it again if Parker was on the line. "I need you to trust me, Bess."

She glanced up at him. "I do trust you. I told you that."

He closed the door to the bedroom as soon as they were inside, turning to face her. "I don't want you trying to take Chris on like that again."

Her chin lifted in a move that he knew well and expected. "I will if I have to."

"You have Parker to take care of. He needs you."

I need you.

It was the part he couldn't say to her. Not yet.

Bess stared him down. "If it comes down to me or him, the answer will always be me, Wade. Always."

Fighting her was futile. His only option was to make absolutely fucking sure that was never a choice to be made.

Because no matter what, the answer would never be Bess.

Or Parker.

It would always be him.

There was a sharp rap on the door at his back. A second later it opened just a crack. "Charles is here. He's ready to sit down with you guys."

"We'll be out in just a minute." Wade rocked Parker a little as Bess disappeared into the closet. When she came out the pajamas she slept in were gone, replaced by a pair of fitted jeans and an oversized pale pink sweater. Wade caught her by the front of it as she came close, pulling her in. "I love that color on you, Sweetheart. Makes you look so sweet and innocent." He caught her lips with his in a quick kiss before continuing. "Makes people think you're not dangerous as hell."

Her mouth quirked in a suppressed smile as she shouldered out the door ahead of him. When they walked into the office Charles was already spreading papers out on the table in front of him. He glanced up as Wade and Bess walked in, shooting Wade a shit-eating grin before turning his attention to Bess.

"This is the infamous Bessie Hines." He reached one hand out. "It's nice to finally meet the woman who has every man on this team a wreck."

Bessie's brows lifted as she shook his hand. "Because?"

Charles slid down into his chair, unbuttoning the expensive jacket he wore over a well-cut button-up. "Because they are ready to slaughter anyone who tries to get close to you and little man here." His smile was warm as it stayed on Bess long enough to warrant a conversation after this meeting. "Apparently you've made quite the impression."

Bess snagged one of the papers with the tip of a finger and slid it across the table, eyes scanning the page as it moved. "What is this?"

"That is the document I filed yesterday afternoon that includes the actual paternity test results showing Wade is without a doubt Parker's biological father." He scooted another set of pages her way. "This is the motion I filed to dismiss Mr. Snyder's claims of paternity toward Parker."

Bess moved from the first set to the second, her fingers moving down the page. "Does Chris know these have been filed?"

"Unfortunately, Mr. Snyder has jumped bail and the courts are currently uncertain of his location."

Bessie's eyes jumped to Charles. "He's here. In Brisbane."

"I didn't hear that." Charles kept going, not giving Bess a chance to repeat herself. "I did speak with his attorney yesterday and he assured me he would be leaving a voicemail on Mr. Snyder's cell informing him of the change of circumstances."

Charles' eyes moved to where Shawn was sitting quietly at his side. "Do you want to tell them the next part?"

Bess looked from Shawn to Charles. "What's wrong?"

"Nothing's wrong, Bess." Shawn rested his arms on the table and leaned forward. "I want all this to be wrapped up quickly. The faster we get this situation resolved, the faster you two can go on with your lives." Shawn paused, giving Bess a minute to process before finishing. "We need to flush Chris out of hiding."

Bessie's gaze was wary. "And how do you intend to do that?"

Shawn reached for the final stack of papers sitting in front of Charles and skimmed them across the table until they were directly in front of Bess.

"I think you two should get married."

CHAPTER 18

"THIS IS AN application for a marriage license." Bess stared down at the paper in front of her before looking up at Shawn and Charles. "You're serious."

"I think it will piss Chris off enough to make him act without thinking. We can do what needs to be done, and the situation will be over." Shawn lifted his shoulders and let them drop. "Done."

"You fill that out, Shawn notarizes it, and I submit it to the courts." Charles' lips tugged into a smile. "Then I'll call his attorney to be sure he knows it's happening."

"So we won't actually be getting married." The realization sat a little strangely in her stomach.

Marrying Wade hadn't crossed her mind.

Not really.

Maybe in a few late night fantasies when she was sitting up alone with a crying baby, trying to find some way to dig out of the hole of depression she was always staring into. In those dark, silent moments, Bess would imagine having him at her side. A man who was strong, and solid, and reliable.

And not crazy.

That was the most important part.

Wade leaned over her shoulder to look at the application. "I mean, I guess it depends on how long it drags out, right?"

Bess couldn't hide her surprise at Wade's question. "We might actually have to get married?"

Shawn shook his head. "I'm banking on this pissing him off immediately. If not, then I should probably retire because I've lost my touch."

"So we won't have to get married." Bess could feel Wade watching her from his seat at her side.

"No." Shawn's eyes bounced to Wade before coming back to her. He gave her a grin. "Not unless you want to."

Bess ignored his last comment and plowed through the plan Shawn and Charles were proposing. "So you want us to submit an application for a marriage license we have no intention of using, because you think it will piss Chris off enough to make a mistake so you can catch him."

"Something like that." Shawn leaned back in his seat. "What do you think?"

It wasn't the worst idea she'd ever heard. And it took the focus off Parker and put it right on her.

The whole time Bess suspected it wasn't really Parker Chris was after and she would like to keep it that way.

He wanted to punish her. It's why he tried to kidnap her son and why he was working so hard to force her to let them give Parker a paternity test.

So he could be a part of her life forever. Making her suffer until the day she died.

"What if we file to have Parker's last name changed?" Wade barely glanced her way. "Add fuel to the fire."

Shawn's eyes rested on Bess. "It's an idea. Is that something you would be willing to do, Bess?"

Her head was spinning. This was all happening so fast. For what felt like forever she'd been praying for a way to get Chris out of her life. Now it seemed to be happening at a breakneck speed. One that left her feeling a little disoriented and uncertain.

Bess rubbed her eyes, trying to buy a little time for her feelings to catch up to the conversation. She liked to think her way through things. Feel the emotions that came up and work out how she really felt.

Usually alone.

But she hadn't been alone in days. Maybe that's what was wrong. Being around so many people without a second to herself was bleeding her dry.

"I don't know that he would care about that so much." Parker had been her son and her son alone for over a year. She was his everything and he was hers. She made all the decisions. Did anything it took to keep him safe.

And now here were all these people, taking that from her.

Did she really even know any of them well? Did they really have Parker's best interests at heart?

What if they did this and Chris found a way to get Parker?

He would kill him knowing it would fill every breath she took for the rest of her life with immeasurable pain.

"I can't do this." Bess shoved up from the table, grabbing her son and pulling him out of Wade's arms. She held him close as she ran from the office and escaped to the only place where no one could get to her.

As soon as the lock on the safe room was flipped she slid to the ground, holding her son against her chest.

He'd been the reason for everything she had done. Every choice she made. Every breath she took.

And now they were using him as a pawn.

Her head fell back against the wall, tipped toward the dropped ceiling of the small space. Bess closed her eyes and took long, slow breaths, pulling in the sweet smell of her baby with each inhale.

She'd done this a hundred times. Maybe more.

Sat with Parker held close, breathing in his scent.

Reminding herself.

This was all for him.

One more deep breath and she pushed up from the floor, ready to go back to battle. Flipping the deadbolt, she yanked the door open and almost fell back.

"Bess, I—"

Wade's toes must have been touching the door, that's how close he was.

And the look on his face nearly broke her heart.

But this wasn't about him. Not right now.

"I need to go talk to Shawn and Charles." She pushed past him, steeling herself against the sadness in his dark eyes. She hurt his feelings, clearly.

He was going to have to suck it up for a minute.

Bess hurried into the office where Shawn and Charles were still sitting at the table, leaned close in a quiet conversation she was about to interrupt.

They'd get over it.

"The marriage license is fine, but I'm not drawing any more attention to Parker. Not now." She peeked over her shoulder as Wade stepped into the open doorway. "I don't want Chris to ever think if Parker weren't in the picture things would have been different."

Oh, God.

What if that was it?

What if he blamed Parker for the fact that they didn't reconcile? What if Chris believed the reason she wouldn't take him back was because she was pregnant with another man's baby?

And that if Parker was gone she would reconsider.

Maybe he wasn't trying to simply kidnap Parker that day.

The realization sat like lead in her stomach, heavy and nauseating.

"We shouldn't have told him about the paternity test." Bess felt lightheaded as the room started to spin a little.

Proving Chris wasn't Parker's dad seemed like the logical solution. Then he had nothing to use against her. Nothing tying them together.

"It had to be done, Bess." Shawn's voice was stoic. "This needs to end before anything else happens and someone gets hurt."

Her eyes narrowed at the men across the table from her. "Wade already got shot."

Charles' red-brown brows shot up. "Shot?" His blue eyes went to where Wade stood. "Did we change the definition of shot since I was here last?"

"I don't care what you idiots call it, he was shot." Bess glared at the man trying to downplay what happened to Wade. "A bullet pierced his body. That's shot in my book."

"If you're going to be one of us, then you might have to update your book, Hines." Charles stood from his seat, collecting the papers strewn around the table. He left the application for a marriage license where it was. "Fill that out tonight and have someone bring it over to me along with copies of your driver's licenses. I think I can get it without birth certificates." He clipped his briefcase shut and slapped Shawn on the back. "Keep me posted. I'll do what I can from my end." Charles gave Wade a matching slap as he passed through the door. "Good luck, buddy."

246

Wade nodded, but his mood was definitely off.

Unfortunately, she didn't get the chance to even breathe in his direction before Shawn was on his feet. "Grab a couple seats. Everyone should be here by now." He poked his head out the door. "We're ready."

Dutch and Harlow came in first. Harlow glanced Bessie's way, an odd look on her face.

Something was wrong.

Bess didn't get the chance to talk to her either, because Shawn was right. The entirety of Team Rogue filed through the door, one after the other. Brock sat beside Wade. Reed and Tyson sat across from her. Nate and Abe sat at the far end with Jamison and Rico came in last, sitting on her free side. Shawn stood at the head of the table behind Dutch and Harlow who already had their computers out. "Remember how we all thought this wasn't just about Bess?"

The men around the table nodded.

Shawn switched on the overhead projector. "We were right, but our guess about who else was targeted was wrong."

Bess looked to Wade.

They thought someone else was being targeted?

He leaned in. "We thought the professional team might have had something to do with your father's business dealings. We thought maybe there were two separate individuals targeting you by sheer coincidence."

"My dad is the most honest man I know." The thought that he might have been involved in something that would put his family in danger was almost laughable. "And there's no such thing as coincidence."

The words were out of her mouth before Bess realized the room had gone silent. Quiet enough that everyone heard her opinion of their hunch.

"And that right there is why I want each of you to beg Hines to move her ass up here and come on staff as a strategist for Alaskan Security." Shawn glanced to Wade and shot him a grin. "I expect some of you to put more effort into that than others."

Bess turned to the man beside her, lowering her voice this time so he would be the only one to hear her next words. "Did he just suggest you try to convince me to stay with sexual favors?"

"That's how I'm taking it." He caught a bit of her hair and slid it between his fingers. "Not that I'm unwilling to offer other incentives."

"I know you're up each other's butts right now, but I need you to listen for a minute. You can whisper in each other's ears later." Shawn reached across Dutch to click the mouse of his computer. A still of the video taken the day Wade was shot flashed onto the screen. "We have reason to believe that Bess was not their intended target." He glanced up from the computer. "We were."

Bess shot up from her seat. "What?"

Were these guys idiots?

Shawn straightened. "You disagree, Hines?"

"Hell yes, I do." She pointed at the screen where a team of five men were scattered across the snowy landscape, tucked behind trees, almost completely hidden in their white gear against the blinding snow. Her eyes snapped to Wade. "You said there's no way one of them would have shot at me by accident."

Wade's gaze held hers. "I did."

"You said you would never have taken a shot at someone if you weren't positive it was who you intended to hit."

"That's true."

Bess turned back to Shawn. "Do you believe the team that shot at me is less capable than this group?"

"I hope they are."

"That doesn't answer my question." She barely shook her head. "Actually it does."

This team was just as skilled as the men around her.

That was the problem.

"Why would they be targeting you?"

"In the past we've dealt with very dangerous people, Hines. Both our clients and the people we were protecting them from. This team has made more enemies than we can count." Shawn pressed both palms into the table and leaned against them. "It was only a matter of time."

Bess glanced around the table. "But there are ten of you. Why would they only send five men out?"

Shawn's head slowly dropped. "Fuck. She's right."

"Nothing is a coincidence." Bess eased down into her chair. "If they were after you they wouldn't have shot at me."

"Unless they are soulless bastards that don't care who gets hurt." Brock was leaned back in his seat, spinning the leather chair from one side to the other.

Was that a possibility?

Bess looked to Wade. His eyes wouldn't meet hers.

A heavy weight settled in her stomach.

This is why he left her. The reason he'd decided never to find her, no matter how much he wanted to.

Because of shit like this.

"So they hacked your system." Bess turned away from Wade.

He might not have wanted her to end up in the middle of his life, but here she was.

And damned if she was going anywhere now.

Bess focused on Harlow. "I don't know shit about hacking, but did you find anything that might help figure out what's going on?"

"Whoever got in was very experienced and careful. There wasn't anything to track back to them." Harlow lifted one finger, halting Bessie's disappointment immediately. "But that alone tells me something." She yanked the cord from Dutch's computer and plugged it into hers, changing the display flashing from the projector to her screen. "There aren't many people who could do that." Harlow's lips twisted into a wry smile. "And I know most of them."

Rows of names stacked down the screen.

"I can't help but notice that most of them are men." Dutch didn't look Harlow's way.

"Lucky us." Harlow clicked to the next screen. "Means ego will work in our favor."

On the next screen Harlow had notes next to some of the names. "These are the hacker's I've dealt with personally. Some of them I think can be eliminated right out of the gate. Some I could see working for a lawless group. A few would pay money to play with people doing bad things." She squinted up at the screen. "I also have a few lines cast to see if I'm missing anyone. Hopefully I'll catch something interesting."

Dutch was staring at her.

Harlow looked at him out of the corner of her eye. "What?"

He shook his head, lips pressing into an approving line. "Impressive."

"For a girl." Harlow's chin lifted.

"Christ, Mowry. Get over yourself."

Harlow's head snapped toward the man beside her. "Kiss my ass, Dutch."

Dutch leaned close enough Bess couldn't hear whatever he whispered into Harlow's ear.

Whatever it was had her skin flaming, either in anger—

Or something else.

Something that probably pissed her off more than Dutch ever could.

"So Harlow is trying to find our ghost team's hacker." Shawn turned to Dutch. "Scour every bit of the footage we have of them for anything that might help us." He pointed around the rest of the room. "I want everyone with their ears to the ground. Touch base with our past clients. See if anyone is having issues that might be relevant."

"This involves me somehow. It has to." Bess stared at the names on the projector. "It doesn't make sense otherwise."

"It might be a coincidence, Hines." Shawn started sliding files across the table, shooting a few at each man.

"Coincidences are like unicorns. They only exist in the imaginations of people who don't look at facts." Bess stood. "I'm telling you, this is connected to me, and if you don't work it like that you'll be sorry."

Understanding people was something she'd always prided herself on. Looking at their behaviors and motivations. Maybe in a different world she would have gone into psychology, but working for the family business was never an option.

It was a given.

And it made sense. She made good money. She helped her family.

It was just boring as hell.

Until two of their fired contractors stalked her and were then murdered by her ex-boyfriend.

Bess was almost out the door when something occurred to her.

She turned to Shawn. "What did the police say about Rodney and Dennis?"

Shawn looked to Wade.

Wade stood from his seat. "Come on, Bess. It's time for us to have a talk."

She barely waited for the bedroom door to close before the questions started coming. "What the hell else don't I know?"

Wade shook his head. "It's nothing like that, Sweetheart." His shoulders lifted and dropped on a deep breath. "The police don't know about Rodney and Dennis."

"What? Why?" Two men were murdered for God's sake. How did the police not know?

"Because no one has called it in yet."

"How is that possible? Why wouldn't you call it in?" Chris killed two men. Surely he wouldn't be able to escape those charges no matter who his father was. "That would put him in jail for the rest of his life."

"We don't follow the same rules as everyone else, Bess." He eased closer. "And I have no intention of Chris spending the rest of his life in jail."

CHAPTER 19

"YOU CAN'T JUST kill him." Bess fought the urge to scream at him.

She understood the feeling. She'd wanted to kill Chris for over a year.

That didn't mean she could just go out and do it.

"What happens if you kill him? Then you go to jail for the rest of your life." Bess rocked Parker, using the motion to soothe herself as well.

Because the idea of losing Wade again was getting more painful with each passing breath.

He shook his head side to side slowly. "Nothing happens. No one will ever find him."

"You don't know that. They find everyone now. Don't you watch television?"

"I don't." He crept closer. "But Alaska isn't like where you're from, Bess. It's why we operate here." One hand came to palm her hip, keeping her from backing up from his advance.

Not that she was going to do that.

"We bring the men we're hunting to us, Bess. That's why your father sent you here."

The comment made her pause. "My father knows what you do?"

"It's why he sought us out, Bess. Because he knew we would handle this the way he wanted it handled."

Her father was the kindest, sweetest, most generous man she knew. "He wanted you to—"

Bess couldn't even make herself say the words.

"When Chris took Parker, what were you planning to do to him?" He wasn't really asking her. Wade knew damn well what she planned to do to Chris.

Had tried to do to him. Unsuccessfully.

"That's different."

"How?" He smiled a little. "You don't think your father felt the same way you did when he found out that Chris hurt you?"

Her father was so calm. So steady. His presence had been a godsend over the past two years.

Never once did he seem to lose his cool.

Wade leaned in, letting his lips trail along the line of her neck. "Your father wants Chris dead almost as much as I do."

"I want him dead the most."

"Not true, Sweetheart." Wade's lips barely brushed her ear as he spoke, one wide palm flattening along the curve of her ass. "No one wants that bastard cold in the dirt more than I do." He lined his body against hers. "He took my son and hurt the mother of my child." His free hand caught her arm, his thumb skimming over the lines of scars from where she and Chris fought over the knife she planned to sink into his chest. "The best thing he could do is disappear. Change his name. His face. Because if I ever find him I will fucking bury him."

She should be ashamed that the only part of Wade's plan that upset her was the risk to him. "What if you get caught?"

"If I didn't know better I'd think you were worried about me." His words carried a trace of a smile.

"Of course I'm worried about you." She tipped her head to one side, giving Wade a little more room to continue nipping his way across her skin. "You're my son's father."

His gentle bites stopped. "Is that the only reason?"

No.

But so many things had changed so fast. Admitting any more of the feelings she was harboring felt like a bad idea.

It felt more dangerous than anything she'd ever done. And she'd jumped on a moving car.

"Bess." Her name was barely a whisper. So soft but filled with something shocking.

Need.

"Please don't make me say it. Not now." Shutting down was so much easier than trying to navigate the truth of her emotions in the chaos currently filling her life.

Analyzing other people was easy. Seeing how they felt through their actions was so simple it was funny sometimes.

Her own emotions had never been as easy to untangle.

"You're making this something it's not." Wade straightened, looking into her eyes with an unwavering gaze.

"What is it?" She always stood on her own. Even when surrounded by her family, Bess always chose to keep most things to herself. Her hopes. Her fears.

Never had she wanted to share them with another person. Not even Cricket, and she told her best friend more than anyone.

But right now she wanted to tell Wade everything.

Even the parts that terrified her.

Like how she might be falling in love with a man she'd only spent a few days with.

"It's easy, Bess. It always has been with us." Wade leaned in, pressing his forehead into hers and closing his eyes. "You were the first person I ever wanted to talk to. I wanted to tell you everything that first night. Explain why I couldn't stay. Why I had to leave you." His hand came to rest against her cheek. "You are like a fucking drug to me. One hit and I was gone."

Bess stared at his face, trying to find the courage to do something that should be so much simpler than it felt. "I—"

"Shhh." His lids lifted. "You don't ever have to tell me anything until you're ready." His lips brushed hers, so soft she almost couldn't feel it. "We have nothing but time, Sweetheart."

Time was such an arbitrary thing.

She was with Chris for five years, and looking back she never really knew him. Not even a little bit.

He was a stranger.

She'd spent less time with Wade than it takes for milk to spoil, and somehow it felt like she'd known him forever.

But what if she was wrong again? At one point she thought she knew Chris.

And nothing could have been farther from the truth.

"I'm scared, Wade." It was the only part of how she felt that Bess could make herself admit, but it was a huge part.

It was something she'd never admitted feeling to anyone.

Not her parents.

Not Cricket.

No one.

"I won't let him near you, Bess. Not ever." Wade's lips moved against her temple as he tried to comfort her.

"No. Not of him." As crazy as it was, Chris no longer scared her. Probably because she knew Wade was telling the absolute truth. He would never let Chris near her again.

But that was the problem. She believed Wade.

She'd believed a man before.

And that went to shit.

"I'm scared of you."

She expected him to be hurt by the comment. Maybe a little irritated.

Wade smiled. "I'm happy to keep proving you have nothing to be afraid of." He pushed against her, backing Bess toward the bed. "It's Parker's nap time."

He was right. In only a few days Wade had stepped in seamlessly, shouldering more than his share of Parker's care. "It is."

"Maybe you should put him in his crib for a while." Wade's eyes went impossibly darker. "So I can get started convincing his momma not to let our marriage license expire."

"Wade, I—"

One finger pressed against her lips. "I won't ever force you into anything Bess, not ever. You're in charge, remember?" His lips quirked into a smile. "But I'm not holding back when it comes to how I feel, Sweetheart. Not after I almost lost everything."

Everything.

Is that really what he thought of her? That she and Parker were everything?

Shit. She believed that too.

Bess blew out a long breath as she carefully laid Parker on the mattress of his portable crib then straightened to face Wade. Just looking at him made every part of her body warm.

Made her feel safe.

She was screwed.

"You better not be faking anything, Wade. I'll kill you." Bess bumped her body into his.

"I'm a big man. We're not easy to hide, Sweetheart." His eyes barely sparkled in the dim light as the sun started to end its brief appearance for the day.

"Harlow would help me." She couldn't stop the smile fighting onto her lips.

"I would imagine Harlow wouldn't be the only one to offer their help if they thought I was treating you wrong." He smiled back at her. "You probably wouldn't have to lift a finger."

"That makes me feel a little better." She pressed her hands to the center of his chest.

"Good."

Without warning, Wade caught her around the waist with both hands and lifted her up, dropping her onto the mattress. "I want to always make you feel better." He quickly shucked his shirt before crawling onto the bed over her and running his nose alongside hers. "I just want to make you happy."

"Why?"

She'd never once offered to make him happy. Hadn't even really considered it.

Because she might be terrible.

This man was willing to kill for her, and she couldn't even take the time to worry about his happiness.

"Because we've both been sad for too long." Wade pressed her back. "And I want you to be as happy as I am."

"You're happy?" Bess fell back against the mattress, holding on as they went down.

"I'm fucking ecstatic." He caught the hem of her sweater and lifted it up, the heat of his skin soaking into hers as their bare bodies pressed together. "I have everything I wanted for the past two years." His eyes moved to where Parker slept in his crib. "And then some."

Bess waited until his gaze came back to hers. "You didn't want to be a father though, did you?"

Wade was silent for a second. "No. I didn't."

She nodded. "That's what I thought."

****

"MY FATHER DIED when I was very young." Wade spent his whole life acting as if it didn't matter.

He never knew his dad, why should it really matter?

But it did. More than he ever wanted to admit.

Now there was no denying it.

It was the reason he chose the life he lived. One with no attachments.

There was no one to suffer if he was gone. No one to struggle because of him.

He knew what it was like to grow up without the man who was supposed to shape you.

That alone shaped him as much as a father ever would have.

Bess was quiet, her hazel eyes soft and sweet as they stared up into his.

Waiting.

For the honesty he would hopefully someday have from her.

"My mother tried, but there wasn't enough. Not ever." Wade slid his fingers into the silky strands of Bessie's hair, using it to ground him as he went back to a time he'd worked so hard to pretend didn't matter. "I saw what it did to her, losing him. I never wanted to do that to someone else."

"She must have loved him very much then."

It was the part of the equation Wade never considered. "I would think."

There were photos of his father everywhere. Even now, all these years later, his mother had them sitting all over the small house he bought her in Florida.

"Did she remarry?"

He shook his head. "No."

His mother had a full life now. He'd made sure of it. She didn't want for anything.

"Do you see her much?"

"No. I don't want to risk anyone tying her to me." It had been years since he'd seen his mother. Dutch put money into her accounts every month and made sure the taxes were paid on her place, all with funds that couldn't be traced back to him.

Bess frowned at him. "You like to decide what's best for people."

"You've seen the life I live Bess. You can't tell me she would want that showing up at her door."

"I can tell you she would love to see *you* show up at her door." Bess shook her head. "You are all she has, Wade. Do you think she doesn't miss you?"

That's exactly what he thought. "I've been gone for years."

"That's even worse." Bess pressed her palms to each side of his face. "When this is all over you're going to go see your mother and introduce her to your son."

"I'm not sure that will make her as happy as you think it will."

"Stop it." Her tone was sharp. Strong. "Stop deciding what people will want and what's best for them."

He'd done it for so long. Starting as a kid, barely big enough to realize he was the man of the house, trying to be careful his mother never knew the weight he shouldered.

"I don't want her to get hurt, Bess."

She rolled her eyes. "Wasn't that your reasoning for walking away from me?" Her brows lifted. "And look how that worked out."

"You're difficult, you know that, Sweetheart?" Wade eased in a little closer to the woman who rocked his world from the first second, taking everything he thought he wanted and turning it upside down.

"I told you I wasn't perfect."

"Oh, I didn't say that wasn't perfect." Wade went back to work pushing her sweater out from between them, this time skimming it over her head and down her arms. "I just said you were difficult." He leaned down to suck at the fullness of flesh pushing up from the cup of her bra. "I happen to like difficult."

She laughed low and soft. "I think you might be a little off your rocker, Mr. Denison."

Wade licked his way up her neck as he worked the clasp of her bra. "What was your first clue?"

"Probably when I found out you killed people." Bess didn't sound upset by the knowledge. It was a simply stated fact, said the same as if she were listing the color of his hair and eyes.

"Don't knock it. I've taken some very bad men out of this world, Sweetheart." The fastener of her bra gave way and he looped it free, setting it on the bed beside them. "I'm hoping to add one more to the list soon."

"Mmm-hmm. We'll see."

Once more, Bess didn't seem upset by the thought.

Finding someone who would know the complete truth of who and what he was had never been a possibility Wade considered.

Because he was sure it could never happen.

But once again Bess proved him wrong.

"Maybe we can go see my mother." Wade found the button to her jeans and flipped it free, pushing down the well-worn pants as she smiled up at him.

"Smug little thing, aren't you?"

"Sometimes." One pale brow lifted. "Still think I'm perfect?"

"Fuck yes, I do." Wade ran one hand up the outside of her leg, lifting it to wrap around his back. "I'm not always wrong, Sweetheart." He snagged a condom from his pocket before working down his own pants, lips finding one pink-brown nipple.

Bessie's hands fisted in his hair. Her back arched under him. Soft sounds passed through her full lips as his mouth worked her breast and his fingers found her pussy.

"I thought of this every damn night, Bess." He circled her clit with a light touch, planning to carefully work her up until she begged him to fill her.

"Fucking me?"

"No." His fingers slid into her, stroking slow and even. "Making you come." He pressed his thumb to the tiny bit of swollen flesh. "But in my head you always said *my* name."

"That's funny." Bessie's grip on his hair tightened, pulling his eyes up to meet hers. "I imagined the same thing."

Wade groaned into her mouth, falling against her soft body.

He was lost. Fucking unfound.

And it's exactly where he wanted to stay.

"Please, Wade. I want you inside me." Bess grabbed at him, trying to get him closer as he patted down the bed for the condom he'd already dropped, dying a little with each passing second he wasn't giving her what she needed.

The edge of the foil wrapper brushed the tips of his fingers. "Thank God."

Bess laughed. Actually fucking laughed. In the middle of one of the most unique sexual experiences he'd ever had. "You are so—"

Her lips clamped shut.

Wade ripped open the pack and sheathed his ready dick. "What am I, Bess?" He situated his hips, easing them between the soft skin of her thighs.

Her face was serious and her tone was soft. "You're a lot of things."

He slid the head of his cock along her slit, wishing just a little bit that he could feel how wet she was. "Such as?"

"Handsome."

"That's obvious." Wade notched himself against her. "Give me something else."

She skimmed her hands down the center of his chest and back up again, indecision warring in her eyes. She was considering giving him something big.

Something important.

But was scared as shit to do it.

He hated that she was scared of him. That's what it boiled down to. Bess being scared of him and her own judgment. "It's okay. You don't have to—"

"You're a good father." Her eyes slowly lifted to his. "A very good father."

Wade leaned down close. "This is why you're perfect for me, Bess. You know what I need even when I don't." He pressed forward, easing his body into hers until they were completely joined. "Thank you."

She nodded, eyes shut tight. Bess wasn't ready to deal with the emotions between them and he couldn't blame her. She'd spent more than a year scared. Alone.

Never thinking this could be.

And now that it was, she was overwhelmed.

He could give her all the time she needed to come to terms with what they were, as long as she did it by his side.

"Don't leave me, Bess. Don't make me chase you." Wade didn't even try to fight the words as they came out. He'd never win. Bess always had a way of making him spill the truths he tried to hide. "Because I would chase you. Forever. Anywhere you go is where I will go." He caught one leg and lifted it high, sliding a little deeper and pulling a gasp from her lips. "You are meant to be mine. You don't have to say it, but we both know it's true."

She held him tight, moving with him as he continued to tell her all the things he shouldn't.

"I can't imagine being without you. I need you, Sweetheart. Stay with me."

Bess didn't give him the answers he was hoping for, but the way she held him said almost enough.

When she came, he came. Her name a prayer on his lips.

Because that's what she was.

An answer to a prayer he never knew was his.

CHAPTER 20

"WADE." BESS SHOOK him a little, trying to make herself stay calm.

He all but flew out of the bed. "What's wrong?" His hair was mussed and his eyes were wild as they scanned the room.

"Something's wrong with Parker." Her voice barely caught.

She could handle anything. Bullets flying at her head. Pictures of dead men. Being locked in a cabin full of people for days on end.

But something being wrong with Parker was the exception. "His fever won't come down."

"Has he had his medicine?" Wade was immediately at her side, resting his palm against the crown of their son's head.

Bess nodded, trying to keep her chin from quivering.

This was the worst possible thing that could happen. Not just because her child was spiking a dangerous fever.

They were going to have to leave the relative safety of the cabin, and they were going to have to do it with Parker. "I think I need to take him to the doctor."

Wade glanced up at her. "It's the middle of the night, Sweetheart, and he doesn't have a regular doctor here." He pulled her and Parker close, the strength of his body bolstering her in a way that defied explanation. "I think we should go straight to the hospital." Wade pressed a kiss to her forehead. "Get ready to go. I'll be right back." He rushed out the door.

Bess hurried to put on whatever clothes she could find and bundled Parker up in the warmest clothes she had. By the time she went into the great room most of the house was already there. Wade stood at the front of the group, shoving his arms into a heavy coat. "Brock, you and Harlow will leave first with Abe and Nate. Bess and I will leave ten minutes later with Shawn, Tyson, and Reed." He grabbed one of the throw pillows off the couch along with the plush blanket tossed over the back and passed them to Harlow. "Here's your baby. Congratulations."

"Don't put that evil on me, Wade." She rolled the pillow into a tube and wrapped it in the blanket before clutching it to her chest as she glanced Bessie's way. "Whadda ya think? Does it look real?"

"It's only got to fool someone from a distance." Wade shoved a hat down on Harlow's head and started tucking her mass of dark hair under the edge. "You won't have anyone taking a real close look, so as long as you move quick and keep your head down we should be fine." He finished hiding her hair and stepped back. "I think it will work."

"We'll head in the opposite direction. I'll let you know if we have a tail." Brock clapped Wade on the back and pulled him in for a quick hug. "Take care of little man, brother."

Wade nodded, jaw set, eyes sharp as he watched the first group leave the cabin.

All eyes were on the bank of cameras surveying the property as the group of four made their way to one of the black SUVs parked in the driveway. Harlow did just as Wade said, head down, moving at almost a jog, pillow baby clutched tightly to her chest.

"That looks like she's carrying a damn baby, doesn't it?" Dutch never looked away from the screen where Harlow was.

"She's something else, isn't she?" Shawn's eyes moved from screen to screen. "Anyone see anything?"

A murmur of negative responses moved through the remaining men.

"Doesn't mean no one's there." Wade moved closer to the screens. "This is dangerous for all of us. Splitting into smaller teams makes us appear weaker." He glanced Dutch's way. "You guys good to stay here?"

"Gotta be. We've got too much here to be able to pack it up in time and I'm sure as hell not leaving it here." He backed away from the screen. "All my laptops are here. Harlow's stuff is here. We've gotta stay."

"Hopefully Brock's team won't be gone too long. We need to keep this spot heavily manned. They probably know we have a decent amount of intel here and would jump at the opportunity to move in on it."

Bess moved into Wade's side. "They?"

"The team that broke into the other cabins." He checked his watch. "It's almost go time. Anything on the cameras?"

Another negative as the men continued to watch the feeds.

Wade's phone started to ring. He answered it before the first trill finished. "Anything happening?"

His eyes moved to Bess as he listened to the other end of the line. "Keep moving. Get them as far away as you can."

Bessie's stomach dropped. She knew this would be dangerous. It was the reason she'd been trying to convince herself Parker was okay. That the fever would break any minute.

But it wasn't happening. He was only getting worse.

And unfortunately it appeared she was right about the danger this posed.

"Someone's following them already?" Bess couldn't keep the panic out of her voice.

Wade stepped in close, wrapping his arm around her while he continued to listen to the other end of the line. He stood solid and strong against her, the flat of his palm rubbing her back in slow circles.

His eyes suddenly darted to Shawn. "We're going now."

Wade disconnected the phone and pulled Parker from her arms, tucking his small body against Reed's chest before zipping the front of the other man's coat over their son. He grabbed a set of keys off the kitchen counter and pressed a button before tossing them to Shawn. "He's getting close to them, but hasn't rammed them."

"Shit." Shawn took the keys and raced toward the door as Tyson came at her with a giant coat.

"Gotta make you look bigger, Hines." He zipped her up in the giant coat and pulled the hood over her head. "Think tall."

She straightened her spine as long as it went and squared her shoulders.

"Good job." Tyson gripped her upper arms and leaned down to look her in the eye. "No matter what happens you always stay behind me, understand?"

She looked to Wade, who was the only one in the group not wearing one of the white coats. Instead he was decked out head to toe in black. "No." She shook her head. "No. Take that off." She tried to reach for him but Tyson's hold on her was strong.

Wade's eyes were different than she'd seen them before as he strapped a band around one leg and shoved in a sheathed knife.

"You can't wear that in the hospital." Bess fought Tyson's grip as he pulled her toward the door.

"I will take it off when we get there." Wade's hard gaze moved to Tyson. "Get them in the car first."

Tyson grabbed the front of her coat, dragging her attention away from where Wade was tucking his handgun into the back of his pocketed pants.

Then he picked up a rifle.

"Look at me, Hines." Tyson shook her a little, waiting until she finally managed to put her eyes on his. "You gotta get it together if you want to get Parker where he needs to go, understand?"

Bess nodded. "Fine."

"Let's go then." He straightened, dropping the front of her coat. "Walk like a man ready to kill somebody."

She smirked in spite of the situation. "I'll walk like a woman ready to kill somebody if that's okay."

Tyson grinned at her. "That's probably scarier."

She nodded. "You're right."

Bess strode past him, head high, eyes scanning the snowy landscape as she stepped onto the porch. It was unsettlingly silent. Like the blanket of flakes was a sound buffer of sorts. She marched behind Tyson and in front of Reed as they moved with quick steps toward the SUV. The low drone of its running engine and the crunch of their steps was the only sound as the group hurried to load into the sleek Rover.

Shawn was already in the driver's seat and didn't even look up as Tyson pulled open the door and motioned for her to get in. Reed followed behind her, settling into the seat beside Bess and unzipping his coat to pull Parker out as soon as Tyson was loaded into the front seat.

Reed immediately passed Parker over. "The windows are tinted. No one will see him now and I'm sure he'd rather be with his momma."

"Ready?" Shawn glanced up at them. Reed and Tyson nodded, shifting in their seats.

"What about Wade?" Bess looked down at the very sick boy in her arms. She didn't want to deal with this alone too.

Shawn pressed a button and the back hatch of the vehicle started to slowly lift just as Wade stepped out onto the porch. He stood out like a beacon.

Which was the point.

He was the target if anything happened.

His steps toward the car were solid and purposeful. The rifle was held away from his body, making it an obvious addition to his ensemble. One that wouldn't be missed.

Wade turned, gripping the open hatch with one hand as he scanned the landscape before climbing backwards into the back.

Shawn pressed the button again and the door lowered, closing Wade in with them. The second it clicked shut the SUV was moving.

Fast.

Shawn sped down the road at a rate that made Bess want to throw up. Parker wasn't in a car seat. She understood why, but still.

A hand came to rest on her shoulder, squeezing gently. "Shawn is the best driver we have. It's why he's with us." Wade's hand shifted to rest on Parker. "Hang in there, Buddy."

Tyson suddenly turned, his eyes moving from Reed to Wade.

"What?" She was the only one in the car not connected to Dutch. It was definitely on purpose, but Bess had no intention of being completely out of the loop.

Tyson didn't hesitate. "He ditched them already."

"Is it Chris?"

"If it's not then we've got bigger problems." Reed leaned to look between the front seats and out the windshield. "How long?"

"Ten more minutes." Shawn glanced at her in the rearview. "How's he holding up?"

Bess glanced down. Parker was tucked against her chest, eyes open and glazed. The flush of his cheeks was darker, the deep pink turning blotchy.

The engine of the Rover revved as it picked up speed.

The rest of the ride was silent and uneventful.

Bess didn't take a full breath until the SUV pulled up in front of the emergency room. "No one followed us?"

Shawn put the car in park. "He probably went back to the cabin. We were far enough away by then that there's no way he should be able to find us."

"Good." Bess climbed out as Shawn opened her door, his large body blocking the gap.

"Chris isn't our only issue, Bess. Don't forget there's more going on here. You still have to be careful, understand me?"

She nodded.

Maybe they were right. Maybe the other team showing up was a coincidence.

Maybe their arrival had nothing to do with her.

It was about time something went right.

"Ready, Sweetheart?" Wade moved into the spot Shawn occupied, standing tall and gorgeous and perfect.

And as a reminder that something *had* gone right.

"Yup." She tucked into Wade's side, ducking against him as they moved into the hospital. The bright colors and integrated play areas caught her off-guard. "Which hospital are we at?"

"We're at the children's side of The Atrium." Wade moved her quickly to the admissions desk where a woman in purple scrubs greeted them with a small smile.

"Can I help you?"

"Our son's fever won't go down." Wade leaned against the counter, taking the clipboard the woman passed over as he continued answering her questions, including Parker's most recent temperature.

The woman's eyes widened. "Have you given him anything for the fever?"

"He's on a rotation of Tylenol and Advil."

She nodded. "Have a seat. I believe they will be with you very quickly." Her eyes barely shifted to the group of men collected at their back.

Wade took Parker so she could fill out the forms, standing and rocking him as she scribbled through the top page. She was barely half-way down when the door opened and a man in the same purple scrubs called Parker's name.

They filled the small ER room, with Shawn, Reed, and Tyson lining the wall while she and Wade answered questions and held Parker while they started an IV and checked his vitals.

Her heart broke when her son didn't even have the energy to cry over the needle stick.

But Wade was at her side the whole time. The solid force she'd been wishing for.

The partner she wasn't sure would ever be.

Reed, Shawn, and Tyson came and went as the hours passed, but they all stayed. Just as steady and strong of a presence as Wade was.

Because it turned out she hadn't just gained one man who would protect her.

Who loved her son.

She found a whole team of them.

CHAPTER 21

"HOW'D HARLOW HANDLE it?" Wade glanced into the room they'd finally moved Parker to an hour ago. Bess was in the recliner with their son sleeping soundly on her chest. He'd waited until she was situated before calling to check in with Dutch.

"I think that woman might be a little crazy." Dutch sounded impressed by the realization. "She couldn't believe they weren't going to run him off the road."

"Sounds like her." He watched Bess as her hazel eyes drifted shut.

Harlow wasn't the only one who'd hoped for a chance to take Chris out last night on their way to the hospital.

Wade hoped the journey would give him the chance to end this. It was why he dressed the way he did. Not simply because he would be the easiest target, but because it would be pretty obvious who he was.

And he wanted Chris to know who he was.

"Has Charles heard anything from Chris' lawyer?" Wade leaned against the door jamb. They'd been at the hospital for almost six hours and he was in desperate need of coffee and food.

But he wanted to be sure Bess was comfortable first.

"He called about the marriage license. Had a few questions about the validity of the paternity test."

The last part caught Wade's full attention. "The paternity test? What the fuck is he worried about with the paternity test?"

"Dunno. Charles said he was pretty focused on that part."

"Not the marriage application?" Wade rubbed the tightening in his chest.

Bess was worried Chris would focus on Parker. The bastard probably knew it was the way to get to her. It would figure the prick was smart enough to realize how he could hurt her the most.

"Sounded like that was barely a blip." Dutch's voice was muffled for a minute before he spoke clearly into the line again. "Harlow wants to make sure you're taking good care of Bess. Says she'll drain your bank accounts if you aren't."

Wade smiled. "I'd let her."

"I'm not telling her that part. She'll find something else to torture you with."

"She can do whatever she wants." There was only one way to successfully torture him, and he'd done it to himself for almost two years.

It's why he had to tell Dutch something he'd been holding back. "If Bess wants to leave I'm going with her."

Being without her wasn't an option. He'd tried that. It was fucking awful.

And that was before he knew how fucking unbreakable she was.

How determined.

How fearless.

He couldn't go back now. No fucking way.

"We all know that, man. Don't blame you." Dutch paused. "Maybe she'll stay."

"I don't know. She'd never left Oregon before this. Her whole family is there. Her best friend." The only thing in Alaska was him, and Wade wasn't convinced Bess was ready to admit he would be enough.

It was the downside to her cautious, thoughtful nature. She took her time working through things.

And the past two years probably only made it worse.

"I guess we'll find out." Dutch was clicking on his keyboard. "Brock's on his way over there. He wants to check in on our girl."

"Our girl?"

"You know damn well she's ours. Don't fucking pretend like you didn't see that coming." Dutch was silent for a minute.

Which was not a good sign.

Wade waited, each passing second setting him on edge. He turned from the room to face the hall, watching every move of each person passing by.

"Jamison and Abe have a visual on a pair of sleds headed toward the cabin." The sound of his typing grew louder and faster. "I've gotta pull most of the team."

"Do what you have to. Keep me posted." He slid his phone into one of the pockets on his black tactical pants.

Shawn hurried toward him with Reed close behind. "There's five at the cabin."

"Five? Dutch just said two sleds." Wade stepped back as the two men rushed past him to collect their belongings from the room. Bess didn't even stir as they quietly grabbed coats and bags.

When Shawn was close he responded, voice low. "Two sleds at the front but Alpha Team just reported another set of two carrying three.

"Alpha Team? What the fuck is Alpha Team doing involved in this?"

Shawn shot him a look. "This isn't just about Bess, Wade." He started past but Wade caught him.

"Just about Bess? What the fuck is going on?"

Shawn glanced back to where Bess and Parker were sleeping soundly in the recliner. "She brought someone to our doorstep, and now we've gotta figure out how to deal with it." Shawn shouldered past, racing down the hall with Reed at his side.

Wade glanced back at where Bess was tucked under the blanket, sleeping safe and sound.

Who the fuck could she have brought? She was a small-town girl from a good family. Chris was a piss-ant senator's son who hired out-of-work contractors to hunt down his ex-girlfriend.

To their credit, they did find her.

Which was odd since they didn't seem capable of doing much else, including anticipating Chris being off his fucking rocker.

His fingers itched to call Dutch. See if he could find out how the two men who used to work for Bessie's family were able to locate her so quickly.

But Dutch was busy dealing with whatever was unfolding at the cabin along with everyone else.

Wade scanned the hall before stepping back into the room.

His cell started to ring within a few steps. He backed up and answered Shawn's call, keeping his voice low so he didn't wake Bess.

"I left my earpiece. Do you see it?"

Wade scanned the room. The small device was on the tray beside where Bess was sleeping in the recliner. He quickly stepped in to grab it. "Got it."

"Brock walked in the doors a few minutes ago. He should be there any second."

Wade stepped out into the hall, looking up and down the quiet corridor.

A team of five men was circling the cabin where they would be able to access all of Team Rogue's information as long as they were willing to do what it took to gain access, and Wade was betting they were. "I'll run it out to you."

Dutch, Harlow and Nate were sitting ducks, and Brock would probably be at Bessie's side before Wade was even on the next floor.

"I appreciate it, man." The tightness in Shawn's tone told him he was making the right call. This was as bad as he thought it was.

Wade pushed into the stairwell and raced down the stairs. Parker's room was on the fourth floor and he was almost to the third when he stopped dead in his tracks.

Chris stood directly in his path, pointing the silenced end of a semi-automatic right between his eyes.

"So you're the son of a bitch who fucked this all up."

****

BESS SUCKED IN a breath as she jolted awake.

A giant man in purple scrubs froze mid-gloving. "Sorry. I didn't mean to scare you."

She gave him a smile. "It's okay. I think I'm just a little jumpy."

"I can imagine. You're little guy was pretty sick." He leaned in to peek at Parker. "How's he doing?"

"Better I think." Bess rested her lips against Parker's head. "His fever seems to be down."

"Good." The nurse pulled on his other glove and moved the rolling tray away from the recliner. "I hate to ask since you look so comfortable, but I need to check him out."

Bess eyed the badge clipped to the pocket of his scrubs.

The nurse grabbed one of the hand-held scanners each person who came in carried, and pointed it at the barcode stamped just under his picture. As soon as it beeped he turned the screen for her to see.

His face and name were displayed just as they were on his badge.

She smiled. "Sorry. I'm just a little protective of him."

He lifted his gloved hands. "I get it. I'm the same way with my kids."

Bess carefully lowered the footrest and stood. Parker woke up and yawned as she walked to the small rail-sided bed.

"His color looks better, doesn't it?" The nurse moved in to the side of the bed. "Hey, buddy. You feeling better?"

Bess glanced at the empty doorway. "Was there a man here when you came in?"

The nurse looked up from where he was gently squeezing Parker's belly. "You mean the big guy in black?"

She nodded.

"He was here when I went into the room next door, but when I came out a minute later to come here he was gone. Probably ran to the bathroom or something."

Bess shifted on her feet.

Wade wasn't the only one who needed to hit the toilets. She'd been so wrapped up in making sure Parker was okay that she hadn't peed since they got here. "Um." She glanced toward the door then back to the nurse. "Will this take a minute? Would I have time to run to the bathroom?"

Wade would be back any second from his own potty break. She could surely leave for two minutes to empty her almost overflowing bladder.

"Of course." The nurse didn't look away from Parker. "We'll get all his vitals done and he will be all yours when you get back."

"Great. Thanks." Bess rushed to the hall. The quiet made her feel a little better. Wade wouldn't have left if he thought there was any risk. She hurried to the bathroom across the hall and nearly tripped on the plastic sign blocking the entrance.

Closed for maintenance.

Well shit.

She turned and caught a passing nurse. "Where's the closest bathroom?"

The nurse pointed to a solid wood door. "There's one down a flight, just outside the door."

Bess glanced at the door to Parker's room. It would only take a minute. She pushed through the door.

Her stomach dropped as a familiar voice echoed up through the well.

Bess caught the heavy door before it closed and carefully slid it into place, making as little noise as possible.

"This is all your damn fault. They thought Parker was mine until you came in and fucked everything up."

Oh God.

Bess slowly crept down the stairs, trying to get closer.

286

She thought Chris was after her and Parker.

And maybe he was at one point, but it didn't sound like that was the case right this minute.

"No one would have gotten hurt if you would have just left shit alone. Her daddy would have paid the money and it would have all been fucking fine."

"It was never going to be fine. They were never going to get Parker whether I was here or not. Bess would have never let anyone close enough." There was unmistakable pride in Wade's voice. "You would have had to kill her."

"I was planning on it." Chris chuckled. "Her daddy would have paid twice as much when Parker was all he had of her."

A chill ran down her spine and settled in her stomach, the icy bite burning like fire.

That man was crazy.

And he was with Wade.

But unfortunately still alive, which meant there was a reason Wade hadn't killed him.

Bess glanced at the door behind her. Running for help would only get more people hurt.

And Wade would definitely end up dead.

The freeze of fear in her belly shifted in an instant.

Wade was hers. He was Parker's.

And Chris wasn't taking another fucking thing from her.

Before she could change her mind, Bess stood tall and started racing down the stairs, saying a prayer that she knew Wade as well as he claimed to know her.

Because if not, then they were both going to be dead.

Bess didn't slow down when Chris and Wade came into view, even at the sight of a gun pointed right at the man she was finding herself loving a little more each day.

Each minute.

Wade barely had time to turn his head and she was behind him, grabbing for the item she prayed he hadn't left behind.

The cool metal of his gun rested heavy in her palm as she yanked it free of the waistband of his pants and aimed right at the man who could take everything from her.

But he wouldn't.

Because she would sure as hell take everything from him first.

Bess didn't blink. Didn't breathe.

Just squeezed the trigger, watching as his body jerked, the bullet hitting him square in the chest. Chris stumbled back, falling against the wall before sliding down to the ground.

A perfect fucking end to the worst year of her life.

Except hers wasn't the only shot fired.

CHAPTER 22

"NO, NO, NO, no."

Wade caught Bess as she started to sway.

Her eyes dropped to the belly that carried his son.

"Wade. I'm bleeding."

"You're fine, Sweetheart." He took all of her weight as she sagged against him.

"No. I think it seems like this is not fine." Her hand pressed to the spot of deep crimson soaking into the knit of her sweater. "It doesn't hurt."

"That's good." He carefully scooped her up just as the door above him banged open with enough force to bounce it against the cinder block wall of the well.

"Wade?" Brock's voice echoed down the stairs.

"Bess is shot." Wade raced up toward his best friend. "I need help. Now."

Brock held the door open as Wade rushed past him into the hall where his son was recovering from the nasty virus that his little body struggled to fight off. "I need someone! My—"

He looked down at Bessie's glassy eyes and paling skin.

"My wife is shot."

The rooms lining the halls seemed to explode, with purple scrubs spilling out around him.

"Don't leave me, Bess." He pressed kisses to her head. Her cheeks. "You're going to be fine. I promise." He cradled her against him, pushing the strands of blonde hair off her clammy skin. "You have to be fine. I fucking need you. Please."

He held her tight as she tried to pull away. He wasn't letting her go. Not fucking ever.

"Sir." A woman with a surprisingly strong grip pulled at his arm. "We need you to put her on the stretcher so we can get her to the emergency room.

When did the stretcher get there?

Wade looked up and found more than just purple scrubs surrounding him. A swarm of blue-clad masked men and women crowded the spot where he sat on the floor. Brock was right by his side, supporting Bessie's feet, his eyes filled with more concern than Wade had ever seen in the other man.

Except they weren't on Bess. They were on him.

"You've gotta let them have her, man." Brock leaned in, wrapping one arm around his shoulders. "I know you don't wanna fucking do it, but she needs you to keep it together right now."

Wade looked at the nurse urging him to give up the woman who changed his whole fucking world in the best possible way.

She nodded. "She needs to go now."

It took everything he had to pass Bess off. Hand over something so precious to people he didn't know, and trust them to save her. He carefully laid her on the stretcher, catching one of her hands and pressing it to his lips as they snapped the sides in place. He searched the faces around him for Brock.

His friend nodded the second their eyes connected. "I'll stay here with Parker. Go with your *wife*." He gave him a wink.

Wade ran alongside the team, holding Bessie's limp hand as they raced through halls and crammed into elevators. Finally they slowed and the nurse at his side rested her hand on his arm. "I'll take you to the waiting area."

"What? No. I need to stay with her." Wade held Bessie's hand tighter. "She needs me."

"I'm sure that's true." The nurse shook her head. "But she has to go into surgery right now."

Wade's eyes dropped to Bess. For the first time she seemed as small as she was. Tiny and fragile. Nothing like the woman he knew. Her eyes slowly moved to him and she softly smiled, squeezing his hand. "Go."

She was still there. Full of fire and strength. Able to take on anything this world threw at her.

And once again she was having to do it alone.

Wade nodded, trying to swallow down the fear threatening to strangle him. "I'll see you soon,

Sweetheart." He leaned down and pressed a kiss to her forehead. "Don't give them too much trouble."

And then she was gone. Whisked away by the people he had to trust whether he wanted to or not.

****

BESS FORCED HER eyes open.

The cloudy voices around her cleared.

"Hey there." A pretty woman with red hair stood over her, smiling. "You woke up quick."

Bess squinted a little, the dryness of her eyes making the backs of her lids feel like sandpaper. "Thanks." She tried to sit up.

"Whoops." The red-head caught her by the shoulders and pressed her back. "You don't want to do that just yet."

"I do though." She was thirsty. And didn't she have to pee?

Wasn't that where she was supposed to be going?

"Do I have a drink?" Bess looked from side to side.

She was in a bed.

A hospital bed.

"Are you feeling sick?" The nurse stopped where she was typing on a computer and glanced Bessie's way. "Does anesthesia normally make you sick? Your husband didn't know."

"My husband didn't know?"

The woman laughed. "Right? I'm sure you're shocked." She grabbed a thermometer and rolled it across Bessie's forehead. "I'm pretty sure mine doesn't even know my middle name half the time." She glanced at the tiny screen on the device before going back to type into the computer again. "I'll go get him in just a few minutes and bring him back."

"Where is he?" Bess lifted one arm and stared at the line of plastic bands stacked on her wrist.

"Hopefully where I left him in the waiting room. Probably driving the people at the desk nuts." The woman glanced at her. "He was asking them for an update on your surgery every ten minutes."

Surgery.

"Does he know I'm okay?"

"Oh yeah. It's probably the only reason he's not crawling through the heating ducts trying to sneak back here." She leaned away from her computer. "Is he a cop or something? All that—" she motioned down her body, "gear."

"Kinda." Bess swallowed, trying to ease the scratchiness in her throat. "Can I have some water, please?"

"Sure thing." The woman backed up and Bess got a good look at her clothing.

Blue scrubs.

Not purple.

Parker.

"Where is my son?"

The nurse lifted a finger. "I'm sorry. I was supposed to tell you that first. Don't tell your husband I screwed up." She winked. "He is with Brice."

"Brock?"

"Probably."

Bess laughed and a strange sensation rippled through her midsection. She lifted the blanket covering her and peered down.

"You got really lucky. The bullet missed everything important." The nurse stepped out and reappeared a minute later with a large plastic-lidded cup. She pressed a button on the side of the bed and Bess slowly lifted up. "So you should be good as new except for the scar." She held the accordion looking straw in front of Bessie's lips. "It's got ice, I hope that's okay."

Bess nodded as she sucked down as much as she could tolerate before the cold liquid started to make her throat ache. "It's good. Thank you." She leaned her head back against the bed. "I think I shot someone."

The nurse's expression sobered. Her eyes held Bessie's for a minute before dropping as she turned away.

"Did he die?"

An unsettling amount of hope rested in her still-partially-numb belly. Only a bad person would hope someone was dead, right?

The nurse stood perfectly still, back to her. After a few seconds she barely turned her head Bessie's way. "We didn't have any other gunshot victims come into the emergency room today."

Bess swallowed, trying to work through the conflicting feelings eating at her.

Parker was safe. Chris would no longer be trying to take him for whatever horrible, terrible reason he had.

She was safe. She would no longer be the thing standing in his way.

And Wade was safe.

But—

"Did you say you were going to get my husband?"

"Yes." The nurse nodded. "I will get him right now."

She should have asked if Chris was dead earlier. The nurse probably would have sprinted to Wade to avoid that conversation.

Bess leaned, reaching to grab the cup of water from the tray that was just a little too far away.

"What in the hell are you doing?" Wade rushed into the tight space, flipping the heavy curtains back as he practically lunged for the cup. "You are going to hurt yourself." He grabbed the cup with one hand and a chair with the other, dragging it across the floor as he held the straw to her lips.

Bess sipped as Wade's eyes stayed on hers. How much could she drink to avoid the conversation that was definitely coming?

"We're going to talk about this eventually, Sweetheart. You'll run out of water sooner or later."

She dropped the straw and waited while he put the cup back in place.

Wade leaned close, catching one of her hands and pressing the palm against his cheek. He closed his eyes and held his hand over hers. "You scared the shit out of me, Bess."

She stared at his face. "Is he dead?"

Wade's eyes opened. "He won't be bothering you again."

"That's not what I asked." Bess narrowed her eyes at him. Why would no one give her a straight answer? "Is he dead?"

"We can talk about it later." Wade turned his head to kiss the palm of her hand. "Right now I want you to focus on getting better."

"Wade." She didn't even try not to snap at him. She'd been shot. Her son was sick. And she might have to pee. "Is. He. Dead?"

They stared each other down for what felt like forever.

Finally Wade nodded.

Bess let out a breath she'd been holding forever. "Good."

Wade's brows barely lifted. "Killing someone isn't a simple thing, Bess."

She looked from side to side, considering his words.

Maybe something was wrong with her.

Because she didn't feel bad. Not even a little.

"Didn't you tell me the world is better off without certain people in it?"

"Something like that." Wade barely shook his head at her. "I didn't know you were going to take it and run with it."

"It was either him or you."

"You don't know that. I would have found a way."

Bess shrugged. "I found a way first."

"Hey." Tyson's head popped between the curtains. "How's our girl?"

Bess smiled at him. "I was shot."

"I heard that." Tyson stepped into the space. "Bullet went in and everything."

She nodded. "And everything." She blew out a breath. "I killed him."

Tyson watched her closely. "Heard that too."

She bobbed her head, trying to find some sort of remorse. "I don't feel bad about it. Not even a little bit." She chewed her lip, hoping Tyson might give her the truth she knew Wade wouldn't. "Am I a bad person?"

Tyson's head bumped back a little. "Hell no. Right now the whole damn team is pissed you got to be the one to take that bastard out." He jumped a little and quick-stepped to one side as a nurse pushed in beside him. "Sorry." The remorse on his face was short-lived as the tall, full-figured woman entered the room. "Good afternoon."

She shot Tyson a look over one shoulder, a dark brow lifting. "Didn't you say you were her brother?"

Tyson gave her a solid nod. "Absolutely I am."

Bess nodded along with him. "I used to have to change his sheets when he wet the bed."

The nurse laughed loud and long, her head tipped back. "I like you."

Bess smiled at her.

She'd been shot.

She killed a person.

And all she felt was peace.

Finally.

CHAPTER 23

"I SWEAR TO God, Bess." Wade caught Parker as she tried to heft him up. "Go sit on the damn couch and I will bring him to you."

She scowled at him. "I'm fine."

"It hasn't even been two weeks. You are not even close to being fine." He held Parker with one arm and pushed Bess toward the couch with the other. "Just because it didn't hit anything important doesn't mean it didn't hit anything. You need to heal." He waited while she dropped onto the cushions of the large sectional before settling their son into his momma's arms.

She smiled as Parker grabbed at her hair. "I'm so glad you're feeling better, handsome boy."

Wade carefully lowered his body to the seat beside her and held out a snack puff. Parker immediately snatched it away, giggling at Wade's fake upset over the sneak attack as he crunched into it.

He wrapped one arm around Bessie's shoulders. "How'd you sleep last night?"

"Great." She leaned back, trying to move Parker without him noticing. "I really like the new bed."

Wade took Parker and sat him between them so his weight would stop pressing on her still-sore stomach. "Good."

She and Parker were discharged from the hospital over a week ago and he'd brought them to one of the smaller cabins Alaskan Security owned.

They needed time alone together. As alone as it was safe for them to be anyway.

"Morning." Brock sauntered into the kitchen in his underwear and grabbed the coffee pot off the maker. "You guys are up early."

"Shawn is supposed to be coming over for a meeting, remember?"

Brock stared at him over the breakfast bar. "Yeah. So?"

Wade shrugged. "I didn't realize you were coming to meetings naked now."

"I'm not naked." Brock shoved the carafe back in place. "Do you see my dick hanging out?"

Bess opened her mouth.

Wade held one hand up. "Don't answer that." He pointed toward the back of the house where Brock was staying. "No more walking around in your underwear."

Brock cocked one hip as he stood and swallowed down his coffee, making no move to go get dressed.

Bess laughed. "Leave him alone. It's a good way to tell how cold it is in here."

Brock straightened, one hand flying to cover his dick. "What's that supposed to mean?"

Bess shook her head. "It's not a big deal. It happens to all men."

Brock slowly backed down the hall before turning to rush toward his room.

Wade leaned into Bessie's ear. "Have I told you how much I love you?"

She glanced at him. "Not in the past five minutes."

He'd spilled his guts within ten minutes of her waking up after surgery. In front of Tyson and a few nurses. It should have been a private moment, but at that point he would have fucking yelled it across a crowded room.

She smiled at him. "You think Shawn is going to let me go visit my parents soon?"

Wade stilled. "Visit?"

Bess hadn't told him she loved him back. She didn't need to, honestly.

The woman took a bullet for him. That told him all he needed to know.

The only time Bess had ever moved fast was that very first night. It was one single leap in a life full of careful steps.

And that was just fine.

She rubbed her lips together, lifting one shoulder to shrug off the full weight of that one single word. "I know it's killing them to not be able to see me and Parker. Especially with the whole—"

she pointed to the spot on her stomach that bore an angry still-healing wound, "gunshot thing."

Every day he woke up thinking this would be the day she would break down. That the full impact of what Bess was forced to do would finally hit her.

But every night he went to bed holding a woman who had no regrets.

Maybe it was because she knew there was no choice. She had to kill Chris or he would have absolutely killed her.

But it was most likely something else that kept Bess from bearing the weight of the guilt and remorse that plagued most people that first time. Even when they know they're doing what has to be done.

Bess smiled wide at Parker. "You are such a sweet boy." She kissed his head, leaving her lips against his skin as she breathed deep.

Ultimately she killed Chris to protect her son. Their son.

Parker would never doubt what Bess would do for him.

And neither would he.

****

"HE WAS IN bed with bad fucking people." Shawn wiped one hand down his face. "I'm not sure we even know the extent of all the people Chris owed money or favors to. Parker's kidnapping and ransom was his plan to clean up the mess he made."

Harlow was leaned back in her seat, Doc Martin's kicked up on the conference table, her dark eyes focused on Shawn, lips barely twitching at the corners.

Bess eyed her new friend before leaning in. "What do you know?"

Harlow glanced her way and gave her a sly smile.

"Do you ladies have something you'd like to share with the group?"

Bess looked up to find all eyes on them. She turned to the woman at her side.

Somehow they had found themselves a part of this group of almost mercenaries.

And maybe she'd earned her place. She *had* killed a man.

And Harlow was cool as hell and smarter than anyone in here, so they'd be stupid not to include her.

And so far these men were not stupid.

"He was trying to break into the drug trade." Harlow tapped the pen in her hand against the arm of her chair. "Unfortunately he didn't have the funds to be as big of a player as he wanted to be. Probably thought Bessie's family's money would be the key."

"The drug trade?" That made no sense. "He didn't do drugs."

Harlow lifted her brows. "The traffickers don't do the drugs. They sell the drugs." She snorted.

"Which is a shame. They'd clear themselves out way faster if they did the drugs too."

The whole room looked at Harlow.

She held her hands up. "What? Everyone knows drugs will kill you." She pointed the end of her pen Bessie's way. "If Chris had done some of the stuff he was trying to figure out how to smuggle up to Canada you probably wouldn't have had to shoot his ass."

"He was trying to smuggle them into Canada?" Shawn sat up straighter in his seat, eyes flicking to Dutch before moving back to Harlow. "Are you sure?"

She gave Shawn an irritated look. "Uhh—yeah."

Shawn leaned back in his seat, the tips of his fingers pressed together as he stared at the table in front of him.

"That other team was checking you out because the actual players thought you might get in their way."

Bess looked at the men around the table. "Chris wasn't smart enough to figure out how to do this all on his own." She looked to Harlow. "Who was he working with?"

"Someone with really good security." Harlow dropped her feet onto the floor and straightened in her seat. "Thank God Chris was stupid or I wouldn't have been able to find out what I did. I hacked his email in about thirty second and found emails he sent himself from whoever he was working with." She opened her computer and flipped it toward the men around them. "I guess he was worried something would happen, so he forwarded the messages to his personal account as a way to have copies. Like a dumbass."

"But now you have their email, so all you have to do is get into theirs the same way, right?" The heavy weight pressing into Bessie's chest lifted a little.

She thought having Chris dead would make things easier. Expected things to be smooth sailing from here on out.

But while the danger to her and Parker was gone, a whole group of men she was starting to love like brothers were potentially the only thing standing between some very bad men and a lot of money.

Harlow shook her head. "It's not that simple." She rolled the pen between her hands. "I tiptoed around a little, and it looks like if I even get close they will know I'm there." Her blue eyes moved to Dutch. "I didn't think it was a good idea for them to know we were onto them."

Dutch smiled. "Good call, Mowry." He held her gaze until Harlow broke it, eyes dropping back to the pen in her hand.

"So what in the hell are we going to do?" Bess didn't like that no one was tossing out ideas yet.

"We?" Shawn's mouth turned up into a small smile. "Does that mean you're going to take me up on my offer, Hines?" His attention bounced to where Wade sat beside her. "Or is it Denison? I heard you had a husband now."

"He was worried they wouldn't let him stay with me." Bess glanced at Wade.

That wasn't why he'd said it. Completely. She knew that.

But they were less than a month into knowing each other. Really knowing each other.

It would be crazy for them to even consider getting married.

And she'd had enough crazy for a little while.

But that didn't mean they weren't something. And dating just sounded so—

Not enough.

He'd saved her life. She'd saved his.

They had a child.

He loved her.

And she definitely loved him.

****

"I HAVE SOMETHING for you." Bess walked into the room they shared, a paper pressed against her chest.

"Oh yeah?" Wade shifted on the bed, straightening a little against the headboard as he closed his laptop and set it on the nightstand. His eyes raked down the front of the soft drape of her pajamas. "I can't wait."

She stopped walking, dropping her head to one side. "It's not that." Her lips twisted into a smile. "Not *just* that."

His hands itched to grab her as she started walking to him again, the need to have her close almost painful.

He'd almost lost her. Again.

Wade held his arms out. "Hurry up."

Bess carefully eased onto the bed and into his ready embrace. She rested against his chest, shifting around until she found a comfortable position. "You still sore?"

He didn't like how long it was taking for her to heal. They said the bullet she took didn't hit anything important, but apparently that didn't necessarily mean a speedy recovery. Knowing she was in pain killed him, which meant he was suffering right along with her.

"It's getting better." She smiled at him. It was tight enough he could tell she was putting it on just for him.

To ease the guilt he fought every day.

"You should have stayed behind me."

"Then he would have shot you."

"I know." Wade rested his palm gently over the spot where the bullet pierced her skin.

Bess frowned at him. "The gun was pointed at your head." She reached up to run her fingers down the center of his forehead and along the bridge of his nose. "And I like your head the way it is."

They were never going to agree on this.

He should have been the one to take that bullet. Period.

Bess let out a sigh. "Stubborn man." She lifted the paper away from her chest and held it up for him to see.

Wade squinted down at the notary stamp across the bottom. "What is that?"

"It's the paperwork Charles and I submitted to have you added to Parker's birth certificate." She flipped the page, revealing a second document. "And here's the one I filled out to have his name changed."

Wade swallowed hard. "You're changing his name?"

Bess nodded.

"You didn't have to do that, Bess." He pinched the paper between his fingers and took it from her, unable to look away from the line in the middle where three words were typed in a different font.

Parker William Denison.

"I know I didn't have to. I wanted to." Bess rested her head against his shoulder.

He cleared his throat, trying to work around the lump making it hard to speak. "As long as it's what you wanted."

Bess tipped her head back to look up at him. "Well, I thought it made the most sense, considering I'll probably have the same name someday." Her lips pressed together as soon as the last word was out.

Someday.

He would take that.

Wade placed the papers on top of his closed laptop before wrapping Bess in his arms and slowly rolling her body under his. "I love you, Bess. So fucking much."

She nodded. "I know." Her hazel eyes moved over his face, wide and a little scared looking. She blinked a few times before barely shaking her head.

"I love you too." The words were soft and rushed, spilling out of her mouth before it quickly clamped shut again.

"I know that, Sweetheart." He cradled her face between his hands, stroking the soft skin of her cheeks with the pads of his thumbs.

"You do?" She sounded surprised.

"Of course I do." He leaned down to find the little dip just below the lobe of her ear with his lips. He nipped it before moving his mouth against her ear.

"I *know* you, Bess. I always have."

Thank you so much for reading Loss Recovery. I hope you loved Bess and Wade's story. It is one that is very close to my heart and I hope it was able to touch yours.

As I'm sure you've guessed, Alaskan Security-Team Rogue will be an ongoing series that is currently slated to have at least 11 books.

That's right. Eleven.

I can't leave any of our boys behind, can I?